The Edge of Europe

Angela Bianchini

•

TRANSLATED
by Angela M. Jeannet
and David Castronuovo
With an Afterword by
Angela M. Jeannet

University of Nebraska Press
Lincoln and London

Publication of this book was assisted by a grant from the National Endowment for the Arts. Manufactured in the United States of America ∞

Library of Congress Cataloging-in-Publication Data Bianchini, Angela. [Capo d'Europa. English] The edge of Europe = Capo d'Europa / Angela Bianchini; translated by Angela M. Jeannet and David Castronuovo; with an afterword by Angela M. Jeannet. p. cm. – (European women writers series) Includes bibliographical references. ISBN 0-8032-1308-5 (cloth: alkaline paper) – ISBN 0-8032-6171-3 (paperback: alkaline paper) I. Title: Capo d'Europa. II. Jeannet, Angela M. III. Castronuovo, David. IV. Title. V. Series. PQ4862.12 C3613 2000 853'.914–dc21 00-024176

CONTENTS

CHRONOLOGY

1915 Italy enters World War I on the side of the Allies (France and Great Britain), who are at war with Germany and Austria-Hungary.

1918 The Allies defeat Germany and its supporters, marking the end of World War I.

1922 The Italian king Victor Emmanuel III appoints Benito Mussolini prime minister of a new government. The end of World War I leaves Italy in an economic and political crisis, torn by strikes and by clashes among political factions; Mussolini's Fascist Party promises to restore order to the country.

1935 Italy begins a successful attack on Ethiopia. The League of Nations condemns the aggression and imposes economic sanctions against Italy. Hitler refuses to support the sanctions, and, as a result, Italy and Germany draw closer politically.

1936–39 The period of the Spanish civil war. In 1936 General Francisco Franco rebels against the leftist parties that were elected to lead the Spanish Republic. Franco's forces win the civil war in large part because of military support given them by Nazi Germany and Fascist Italy.

1938 Hitler invades Austria and annexes it to Germany. In a show of support for Hitler, Mussolini chooses not to intervene.

Although a significant number of Italian Jews support the Italian Fascist government, Italy makes public its "Manifesto on Race" written by Italian "scientists." One of its statements reads "Jews do not belong to the Italian race." In time Italian Jews are subjected to a series of "racial laws": Jews are forbidden to participate in any international congress or event; all Jewish students and teachers are expelled from Italian schools at all levels, including universities;

foreign Jews who entered Italy after 1919 are expelled from the country; and the "Guidelines for the Defense of the Italian Race" decrees a systematic policy of discrimination against Italian Jews.

1939 On 26 January Barcelona falls to Franco's army, marking the end of the Spanish civil war. Spain's Republican forces are thus defeated, and Franco's Fascist regime is instituted. In September Germany invades Poland; the Second World War in Europe begins.

1940 Italy declares war against France and Great Britain.

1941 After the Japanese attack Pearl Harbor, Italy declares war on the United States.

1942 In Wannsee, a Berlin suburb, the top Nazi Party members draft the "final solution," that is, the concrete plan for the extermination of all European Jews.

1943 The Allies land in Italy. The Italian king flees from Rome to the port of Brindisi in southern Italy. The German Nazis occupy those parts of Italy not yet controlled by the Allies. The anti-Fascist Italian Resistance movement strengthens. The Nazis raid the ghetto in Rome and deport more than one thousand people. By war's end, eight thousand of Italy's forty thousand Jews will be deported and killed.

1945 In April Italy is fully liberated by the Allies. In September Japan capitulates, and World War II ends.

The Edge of Europe

CHAPTER ONE

Arrival

The mid-April afternoon, gray and stormy, came to a close, toward dusk, in the small airport. In the west a gash of bright orange was breaking up the banks of dark lowering clouds, casting an unreal light, heavy with menace, on the short strip of grass where the Ala Littoria plane had just landed with several hard bumps.

When the girl stepped off the plane, the air felt humid and the grass wet, as if from recent rain. In the distance, toward the wooden barracks that housed the police and customs, the silhouettes of a few open umbrellas made a curious border; they were interspersed with the Portuguese *carabineros'* cocked hats, also black but shiny as oilcloth, more Victorian than the uniforms of the Italian *carabinieri* with which she had been familiar until then.

Everything, in a way, seemed familiar but curiously different, just as she had imagined, yet somehow disappointing. For instance, she had expected to see a person who, according to the telegram, was supposed to appear among the open umbrellas and come out of the small knot of people to welcome her. Instead, that person was nowhere to be seen, and perhaps wasn't even there. The name of that person was totally impersonal – Stone, like the name of a character in a detective novel or film. The telegram announcing his acceptance of this mission was also rather mysterious: "Will Be Waiting Lisbon Airport Wednesday 16 April 1941. Reservation Made Pensione Europa. Joseph Stone Journalist." When the telegram had arrived her mother breathed a sigh of relief: "They have been so wonderful. At least you will have some support. Now it's all set, thank God." The telegram was stashed with all the other documents in the pigskin beauty case that the girl held, not by the handle, but tightly under her arm for fear of losing it. As she walked alone toward the police checkpoint, the girl told herself that actually nobody knew this Mr. Stone – neither she (who didn't even know what his face looked like) nor her American relatives who, working through the office of the Jewish Community, had taken the trouble of finding someone to help her. He might not have existed at all. He might have already left.

CHAPTER TWO

At the Littorio Airport

The long, absurd day had begun in the company of a few other passengers in another airport almost lost in the remoteness of the countryside near Rome. When the racial laws had been enacted two years earlier, the girl's mother had fallen from an utterly blind faith in the higher destiny of her country into an anguished and desperate agitation. But that morning she once again became calm and serene, almost happy. The girl's departure was indeed the result of long negotiations aimed at gathering the necessary documents. Feeling the impending threat of the Nazis, the mother had pushed her passive and fatalistic daughter along the bureaucratic route, day after day, month after month.

Each piece of paper, each document obtained had been a triumph for the mother, another step toward her daughter's salvation. For the girl, each document meant one less obstacle between her and a departure she did not want to think about. Only once had the mother been on the verge of wavering, that day in January when the American consulate, having judged the financial coverage insufficient, had refused for the second time to grant a visa. The vice-consul sat upright under the portrait of Roosevelt and the American eagle; anxious pleading carried no weight in the insulated office that overlooked the gray wintry sea of Naples.

"She is so young," the mother had said. "For myself, it doesn't matter, but she must be saved."

"If we had to accept everybody," the consul had answered icily, "there would be no end to it."

The north wind blew just as icily through the streets. Once outside, the mother, who was tall and thin, hunched over as she walked, as if she had become resigned. Then she straightened up: "No," she said, "we must try again, we must send letters to America again."

A month later the visa was granted, and all the other documents arrived as well, one by one.

The morning of the departure at the Littorio airport, the mother seemed to be in seventh heaven, and in the end the daughter found herself envying her mother for that happiness, for her sacrifice, for the serenity of her conscience. Their parting came about with sudden brusqueness, almost immediately after the inspection of the girl's passport, which specified race in addition to name and surname. At that point, the girl had been separated from the small group of passengers; she was led to a darkened room and then searched. Suspecting that she might hide valuables in addition to those she had declared, a policewoman in a black uniform and kepi undressed her. The girl, in those last minutes, tried in vain to erase from her mind the woman's face and those hard hands that searched her with hostility. Then, the three-engine plane approached, and as she concentrated on holding tight to her skirt and her big yellow leather handbag, she felt as if the turbulence caused by the propellers were sucking her into the depths of a storm. Her mind returned to thoughts of death, and she saw the small plane with its innocent appearance as the vehicle of her demise, the "exit" of her (almost) twenty years.

CHAPTER THREE

Madrid

On the aircraft, the passengers were few and quiet in their lonely flight. Down below, the Mediterranean had curled into small, frothy waves, from which islands rose up in relief, as if on a map of the world. Then, after so much blue sky, so much water, so many islands, land had finally appeared. It was almost deserted, devoid of the signs of human presence: mountains, mountains, and more mountains, valleys and forests, the tips of which the tiny plane seemed almost to be skimming.

The mountains were all dark green with some patches of a brighter hue. When the plane made sudden dips, the passengers complained loudly as they felt their stomachs rise into their throats. Still, the plane continued to beat its way as best it could through the mass of sparse clouds that were now thickening. Sometimes it would lift itself above them; other times it dove underneath, cleverly eluding and circling them, as if in a game of hide-and-seek. But there were moments when the weather was not to be avoided: the clouds, now swift as sailing ships, came rushing against the plane and engulfed it. The wings shook, and the aircraft swayed, first right and then left. Its wings, it almost seemed, were each going in a different direction. And then, suddenly, with a great shake and boom, the plane would soar again.

"This is crazy," grumbled a man who was sitting behind the girl. He had been discussing commercial affairs because he was a Milanese businessman traveling to Spain. He got off at Barcelona. The last passengers got off in Madrid, and so did the girl because she had to change planes.

The Spanish airport was fairly large and well set up. And in Madrid, the girl found a restaurant of sorts where she wanted to order some broth. But although she knew it, the Spanish word for "broth" would not come to her mind. It was only when the waiter, more clearheaded than she, set a bowlful down in front of her that she remembered it was called *caldo*. But by then it was too late. It was time to go, so she was not able to finish it.

CHAPTER FOUR

Five Hundred Dollars

The new plane, also flown by the Italian airline, was even smaller, and that increased the girl's fear of falling. Spain came toward her, brown and green, all gorges and mountains wrapped in banks of fog and clouds. To the girl it seemed to be sealed in a sort of silence or slumber, not peaceful but born of oblivion or exhaustion. And as she contemplated that slumber now from up above in that small plane, she felt remorse for having understood little to nothing of the war that Italy had touted as a Fascist war, for having cheered the fall of Barcelona, and for having believed that those lands and those rivers – Toledo, the Hebron, the Asturias, Galicia – were far away. They were near, right below her. After so many battles and so much bloodshed, life perhaps still throbbed there, even if not visible, under that blanket of stormy clouds.

Those lands appeared down below, came toward her, and then slipped away from her with each maneuver of the little plane that flew sometimes level, sometimes banked. Very few houses were visible, isolated against the bare dark brown earth. Now there were only two passengers in the plane, a man and the girl, with the two pilots seated up front, a short distance away in the cockpit. When the weather turned very nasty and the rain, in addition to erasing all visibility, started streaking the windows violently, the copilot came to sit beside her.

Unlike the woman with the black kepi, the airman was quite kind and very much wanted to know what was so precious in the big travel bag that she held on her knees. He was curious about why she had embarked on her journey and if she would be meeting a lover upon her arrival. For more than two years the girl had become accustomed to speaking as little as possible in public and not revealing anything about herself. So she tried to be evasive, to avoid speaking of documents or embarkations. At the same time, she fended off the copilot and was playful and natural with him, as he teased her good-humoredly. He ended up convincing himself that the girl was not traveling just for leisure, but that a fiancé was waiting for her and even that she was going to get married, for the girl had not been able to give him any hint as to the date of a possible return to Italy.

"Well then," said the pilot who smiled with his bright and well-aligned teeth, which seemed almost foxlike under his thin black mustache, "you really don't trust us to fly you back. Are you frightened?"

At that, the girl denied that she was afraid or that she was even in a hurry to arrive, because actually her anxiety about the trip had by this point subsided. She had the impression that she was the only person flying that day above a Europe at war, the only one for whom it was possible to observe everything from the sky – the folds, the ravines, and the brown expanses of the continent. Still, almost without being aware of it, she was tormented by uncertainty about what she would find at her arrival. And having been used to life at home surrounded by people who listened to her, she felt the weight of the realization that for a long time she would not have anyone to whom she could recount the experiences of that day.

Now with the rain came lightning that pierced the large black masses, and the copilot returned to his post. The plane fought courageously against the storm, and everything was pitch dark inside. The girl could make out only the backs of the two pilots. They shouted to her to be brave because they were almost there. She felt nauseous though and on the verge of getting sick at every bump. At the same time, she was no longer very concerned with departures, arrivals, nor even the people she had left behind. She concentrated only on holding tight to the big travel case, which, in addition to the documents, the photos, and her jewelry, contained five hundred dollars.

Suddenly, the plane shot through the clouds and into the sunlight. The joyous golden light invaded the entire sky, and under it the green earth reappeared. It was inhabited now and was neatly scored by trees, trellises, fields, streams, woods, small houses, and even railroad crossings.

They were flying quite low, and the girl noticed a large, green river such as she had never seen before. It was wide and magnificent, and it parted into many smaller rivers that contained and divided the green landscape. Everything shone in the sun of that different world.

“The Tagus. The Atlantic Ocean,” said the pilots. “See, signorina? We are in Lisbon.”

But as to the ocean, the girl did not have time to see it. Of that arrival she would always and only remember the immense majesty of the Tagus.

When she landed, she found the sunset stormy. The plane was over two hours late. The entire April day had been taken up by that flight.

CHAPTER FIVE

Deluxe Refugee

"No, there is no one for you," said the officer who was examining her papers.

Entering the wooden barracks, the girl had the impression that there were some people waiting in a corner, but in her haste to reach the policeman's table, she did not manage to see them clearly.

Now she was standing in front of the long table, her back to the door, facing a man in uniform and another man in civilian clothes. The policeman opened the documents and checked them over, one by one, before handing them to the other man, who was probably an official. To the girl it seemed they acted not only with diffidence but with extreme and deliberate slowness as well. She tried to gather her courage by recalling, as her mother had told her so many times, that she had all her papers in order; but into her mind, at the same time, came all the tales that were circulating even in Italy, of espionage and fear, of the confusion that reigned in Lisbon – the city that was the only gate still open toward the Americas, the only way out of a Europe invaded by the Nazis. She wondered where she might end up if by chance she were not allowed to enter Portugal: surely not in Italy, from which she had, at this point, effectively been expelled; nor in America, because it would be impossible to embark. Back into her mind came thoughts of extradition and even of German concentration camps. Her mother used to speak continually about them – she who in that moment was surely exultant, believing her daughter to be safe.

"And this, what is it?" asked the official. He had her passport in his hand.

"The final exit visa from Italy."

"And what is written over here?"

"That I am a Jew; it is the declaration of the Jewish Community office."

The policeman, and then the official, took back the passport and examined at length the entrance visa for Portugal. That had been the most difficult to obtain because the Portuguese consulate was open only two hours a day, and then it turned out that the consul was always out of the office – and to grant the visa he had asked for a facsimile of the embarkation ticket. When, through a series of fortunate coincidences, it had become possible to enter the consulate and present the ticket that had been sent from the United States, the clerk refused to grant more than four days of sojourn in Lisbon.

"The city is crowded to the saturation point, and you will not even find a place to sleep," he had said.

"Do you know that you have to leave the city on Saturday?" asked the official with an accusatory air.

"I'm sailing Friday evening at five o'clock," said the girl, "and I have a hotel reservation. And they are waiting for me."

"No, there's no one here for you," said the official, handing her the documents in a disordered and confused bundle, in which he had now lost all interest. "Remember, only four days."

While she was still standing there, trying to push the papers back in her bag, recalling that the name of the pensione – "Europa" – was written on the telegram, and deciding that she would take a taxi and manage by herself, the girl felt a gaze on her shoulder. Turning around, she saw a gentleman who was waiting and smiling. He was wearing a gray felt hat with the brim lowered and a trench coat; in his hand, he held a dripping umbrella.

"Mademoiselle. At last," he said in French.

"You are . . ." But before she could say the name, the gentleman had interrupted her.

"Well, shall we go? It is almost six," he said. Then, with a shrug, he added: "They had told me the plane from Rome would arrive at three. Let me carry your bag."

"No, no," said the girl, clutching the big bag she had managed to close again only with great effort. "It's all right, I can carry it."

"As you wish." He gave another quick smile. "Whatever you say. Let me carry your fur then." And he added: "What lovely things. A deluxe refugee."

CHAPTER SIX

Mr. Stone

They were standing at the airport exit waiting for the luggage to be loaded in the taxi. The girl, looking at him furtively, realized that the gentleman's smile was not warm – as she had thought at first – but rather ironic.

"My office was full of people, and I stopped everything to come here to pick you up. I thought I would take care of this in two hours. All I needed was this delay."

"I am sorry," said the girl with a dignified tone.

She was offended by his definition of her as a "deluxe refugee," by his smile and his recriminations. But she felt the need to communicate anyway, to speak about her trip and about herself. She wanted to tell him all about that brown earth, that green, that void, the strange flight with the bad weather and her loneliness – and the vision of Europe that had appeared to her in the storm, in the midst of her loneliness, like a warning. She wanted to tell him that on that very morning she had left a beautiful house and an excellent family that had been the target of racial laws in spite of its patriotic merits. She wanted to tell him about her mother who had sent her away from Italy at all costs. And she wanted to explain to him that his intervention had been sought because she was not yet twenty and was traveling alone.

"How old are you?" he asked, opening the taxi door for her.

"I will be twenty soon. Very soon."

"Good," said he. "Only for that reason do I forgive you for the time you made me waste. And also for the stupid telegram they sent me from America. You could be my daughter." He started to laugh; they were already seated in the taxi. "I have an eleven-year-old daughter. So, you will allow me to call you by your first name."

"You may," said the girl, and without her wanting it to, her reply automatically took on an artificial, worldly tone.

They were sitting next to each other now, and the landscape ran rapidly by the car's window: first, expanses of deserted runways with small airplanes delicately resting on them, and then white cottages and modest gardens, under a still menacing sky. Only a sort of profile à la Jean Gabin was visible of the man, between the hat's brim lowered over his eyes and the trench collar raised on the nape of his neck.

"So, your name is Stone, isn't it? Are you American?"

"No," he said, and he turned his face toward her as he took off his hat.

He showed a dark face, pale and puffy almost like an Asian's. The glance of his black large eyes, deep and velvetlike under heavy, melancholy eyelids held her while he started speaking rapidly and with rancor.

"No, not at all. I am not American, and my name is not Stone. That is just a name . . . a battle name, one of many. I am Russian, from Kiev," and the girl remembered Zangwill's short stories, the only Jewish stories she had ever read. "But I lived in France many years before all this . . . ," and his full lips grimaced with contempt, "before all this mess, Hitler, and all the rest." The girl again thought of Jean Gabin's films. "When Hitler came to power, I was in Germany, actually," he chuckled. "I had fled Russia shortly after the Revolution. Always fleeing either right before or shortly after the storm. It's the Jews' fate. I have had three or four countries. Three nationalities with respective passports."

"You came here from France?"

Taken aback by such an unexpected burst of bitterness, the girl was searching for some familiar hold in that life that had gone on so removed and different from her own.

"Not at all. From Casablanca, when it became impossible to stay on. And then it was necessary to do something to save the others, too. Even people like you, who announce their arrival by telegram." He must have had the impression that the girl had not yet understood, that he had not been clear enough, because he added: "But I spent four years in Spain, too. Almost the entire war. I left in 1939; I was among the last ones. I crossed into France. There, naturally, I did a bit of time in a concentration camp. I had been a journalist, nothing else. That is my trade." And then he added: "My name is Rubin. Jean, or Juan, or Ivan, as you wish, Rubin. Or rather Ruben, as the French say."

When he pronounced his name that way, the girl had a sudden illumination, like a flash in the dark, and saw the phrases "the Cassandra-like Ruben," "the fugitive Ruben," "Ruben the defamer," "the demoplutocratic Ruben" that had appeared in the Italian newspapers through the years, from the time of the sanctions, of Ethiopia and the Spanish war, down to France's defeat; that name was always accompanied by "Eden the coward," "Churchill the buffoon," "the infamous Azaña," and "De Gaulle the traitor." And as she had done when she had glimpsed Spain from the air, she thought: This is History; this is the rest of the world I never knew.

Ruben, rapidly, gave her some information about Lisbon, which was costly and treacherous; and about the Pensione Europa, which wasn't too expensive and was located in the modern, higher section of Lisbon. The Pensione Europa had been chosen because he was staying there with his wife, and also because – and he smiled – they had instructed him to watch over her. He asked her if she still had enough money for her stay or if she needed anything.

"No, not at all," said the girl pointing to the bag. "I have money. And I also have five hundred dollars."

He smiled again: "Right, you are rich. They allowed you to take that money out of the country?"

The girl nodded, and he added more quick questions: How had she obtained permission to export currency, how many people, as far as she knew, did obtain such permission, had she been searched, and were the Jews who might be trying to leave Italy still numerous. When the girl said that no, with Italy now at war for months she thought that she was one of the last to leave, he agreed and said:

"That is true. We were surprised."

At first the girl answered eagerly because she had not spoken with anyone for so many hours and besides, she liked to feel herself the object of interest for a man who was so important and must have been – according to her calculations – at least forty, or even forty-five years old.

Lisbon began to go by, handsome large buildings and piazzas with statues and trees, where the streetlights had been lit and dotted the spring evening. The questioning continued, hammering at the girl, offensive to her ears, as if all Italians were included in Ruben's rancor against Mussolini, and finally she bridled:

"No," she said, "it's not such a tragedy after all. It's not true that Italians lack everything. Of course, there is no coffee and there is no tea either; you can't find soap, and it must be made at home. There is rationing, but fabrics and shoes can be found, and we can still make do, and many have plenty of supplies."

"Many, who?" asked Ruben. "The bourgeoisie, the wealthy. What about the people, the proletariat?"

That was a word the girl did not remember having heard often. As a matter of fact, she had probably only read it, and she was astonished.

There were lots of words Ruben used – "the democracies," "the allies," "we antifascists," "Italy's defeat," "the betrayal of France," and "Mussolini's cowardice" – that she had not often uttered, not because she had hopes or thoughts different from his, but because she had forever been accustomed to using different words, and to remaining silent for many years now. Ruben's insistent and violent questioning was tearing the silence that now spread over Italy. In Italy no one asked questions or answered them because there was always someone who boasted that he wanted to break Greece's or England's back.

The sensation of a void opening up beneath her struck her once again that day, as had happened during her flight. But she also had another sensation, unpleasant and illogical, that with the freedom she had suddenly acquired and was putting to use, she was abandoning all those she had left behind in their silence. With them she had shared her life until that moment, and now she felt as if she were wishing their death. She was tired, all of a sudden, and irritated; she again felt nausea at having left Italy, which she had never wanted to abandon. She answered that yes, the racial laws existed, but patriotic merits also counted, as in the case of her family. Jews had been deprived of radios and domestic help, but they did not at all live in isolation, at least not the ones she knew. The Italians, by and large, were very kind; and as for the Germans, they must certainly have been in Italy, since everybody said so, but they were not very visible.

Ruben did not seem particularly surprised to hear that she was not only ill-informed but also discourteous.

"Ah, you bourgeois Jews," he said. "You always see things too late," and he changed the subject, pointing out for her Lisbon's attractions: the coast, splendid and picturesque, which they had just left behind, the higher and more modern section, where she was going to find the hotel, and the other section, the older Lisbon around the Castle, which was barely visible. It was the girl who asked if the Pensione Europa was far from the shipping company where she was planning to go the following day, to check if her trunks had arrived and to have them loaded before departure.

"I have everything else ready," she said, "ticket, papers, and the declaration of Rome's office of the Jewish Community."

"Good," answered Ruben a bit distractedly. "But there is still plenty of time. Your ship will not arrive before day after tomorrow."

When they were in front of the hotel, the girl asked if he also was going to go in.

"Me? Can you imagine! With all the work I am saddled with and the time I had to waste."

He had put his felt hat on again, and he was looking at his watch with ferocious eyes. But then in the lobby of what was truly a family-style hotel – with rattan tables and armchairs and a bar crowded mostly with men – he wasted more time introducing her to the receptionist, who was doing crosswords behind the desk, and making sure that she had been assigned the right room and a place at his table in the dining room.

"We shall see each other tomorrow. My wife and I are going to dine out tonight."

CHAPTER SEVEN

Pensione Europa

The following morning, as she went out, the girl realized that the hotel was situated very high on a narrow terrace filled with pines, hydrangeas, hibiscus, and oleander. At the back, the area was bounded by a massive crescent-shaped wall, a sort of high-backed bench, and at the front by a long balcony with stone lions.

Two ramps descended from the balcony and met halfway down the slope, looking toward the city. Under the ramps, as Ruben had explained, were the entrances to the large avenues that led to the lower part of town. The avenues were very wide, swarming with people and flanked on either side by trees and flowerbeds. In the middle, cars glided and trolleys rang their bells. Between the flowerbeds and the stately buildings, the crowds, while strolling and chatting, watched the traffic go by. All the buildings were tall and adorned with flowers, turrets, domes, and balconies. Some even had imposing porticos supported by high columns. Under the arcades, which were somewhat dark, were stores and cafés. Their awnings stretched in the open air beyond the arcades, where the avenues widened further into rectangular or square piazzas. Each of the piazzas was closed upon itself like a large salon, with an obelisk in the middle and ornamental flowerbeds at the four corners, in the Italian style, and tall nineteenth-century lampposts all around the perimeter. To the girl's eyes, the piazzas and their avenues looked like sets prepared for theatrical events that were about to happen yet somehow never did. Then, as she walked on, she realized that in the very movement of the crowds and in the air there was an ever-growing feeling of suspense.

A warm, stormy wind was blowing. Toward the hills, clouds, high and swollen, were crossing the sky. As they passed in front of the sun, they threw shifting lights – like changes of seasons – over the city, the crowds, the avenues, and the piazzas. At times the clouds lit up everything with bright flashes. At times they made everything look flat under their moving shadows. Always they stirred ripples, shivers. And everyone seemed to be driven on toward the port and the ocean, as if by a turbulent flood tide.

The girl felt intoxicated by the excitement that was flowing between the tall, majestic buildings and the Atlantic. She had the impression that she had already felt such excitement elsewhere and yet never quite as strong and close as it felt in that city's air, which was riper, more scented, and more vividly colored than an Italian springtime. From the port, which remained totally invisible but could be heard nearer and nearer, there came every so often, carried by the wind, the howling of sirens. It sounded like a nervous call to departures, to crossings, to the unknown. But it was that unknown, it was that departure, now so near, that the girl still feared and from which she recoiled. It was the city she liked, because it was her own discovery, neither foreseen nor foretold by anyone else. She liked that rich yet linear city, enclosed – so it seemed – by the ocean and the hills, watched over and protected by Ruben's hotel.

At last, she felt the temptation to check on her ticket and the trunks she had shipped such a long time before. She wanted to confirm that they had preceded her and that they were waiting for her, filled with the new items, so beautiful and elegant, that her mother had bought her. She asked a passerby for directions to the office of the shipping company.

Beyond a large square with an obelisk at its center, the streets narrowed and became thicker with crowds of people that were ever more colorful and multilingual. They were all elbowing their way and speaking at the same time. The girl wondered how many of those people were waiting for a departure, for a ticket, a ship, or a visa, and how many lived and worked there. But she could not decide, because once again, the city seemed to have drawn to itself and involved all those preparing to leave, all the inhabitants, all the refugees, all the spies, into its nervous rhythm of preparation and anticipation, destined perhaps never to be fulfilled.

Along the narrow streets or alleyways, which were called "ruas" and were flanked by very tall, tightly packed houses, the doors were inscribed with lists of the magical names of all the world's travel agencies – Cook, American Express, American Export Lines, Iberia – which had ceased operations in all the other parts of the world. The girl found among them her own agency too. It was on the main street, also very narrow and dark. Occasional sunbeams slid down between the buildings.

The office, which carried a prestigious name, was also gloomy, old, and hidden away. It was filled with bookcases, desks, and counters made of dark, polished wood. Its glass doors opened at the sound of a gong. It looked as if nothing ever happened there, as if the courteous but sleepy employees, with their soft-spoken English, had had no contact with the outside world for years, nor with the war and the refugees. And yet they were expecting her, they knew her name, and they knew everything about her shipment and ticket. In two minutes, out of those ancient shelves and safes sprang the documents concerning her and her sailing. As had happened at the airport, the girl had the feeling that the safety net of visas and permits so patiently woven for months by her mother extended from Italy to America, across all of Europe, and had now become unbreakable. The set of papers – until recently so far out of reach – was now in perfect order and complete. The ship was to be in the port the following day, the time of boarding was already set, and nothing stood in the way of her going on board two days later at six o'clock in the evening.

"Perhaps," she told the clerk to quiet her last scruples, "I should obtain one more statement from the office of the Jewish Community in Lisbon. Don't you think?"

"It could not hurt."

The reply was laconic, and the girl's conviction that such a step would be superfluous was confirmed.

"I will get this information myself," she reassured the clerk, a young man with dark hair and a long face, named Perez. "I know someone who works there." She then made an appointment with the clerk for an hour before embarkation in order to get the receipts for her trunks directly from him.

As she headed toward the hill to return to the hotel – into the crowd's flow that, instead of ceasing, was now going both ways – the girl felt that the sense of isolation and the fear she felt the evening before had dissolved in the excitement of that day. In fact, they had been replaced by a sense of expectation that involved not the future nor the sea voyage, which she still viewed as undesirable and hazy. It had to do, rather, with those three days that had barely begun, with her sense of independence in the city she had just begun to discover, and with her perspective on the world, which was also new and had been kept hidden from her until then. Just as everyone said, the city was untouched by the war: it did not have the muted, secretive life she had left behind in Italy, nor the large, empty, wounded spaces of the Spain she had glimpsed from the air. Actually, this city was neither at war nor at peace but was throbbing and lively, and resentful perhaps. Like Ruben. If the girl now knew whom to contact and where to return, at least for the next three days, it was due to Ruben. His protection was quite different from the way she had imagined it on the plane, but it was palpable, even from a distance.

Recalling the previous evening, she became aware of how much Ruben was foreign and familiar. He was completely different from the American journalist she had expected to see and whom he resembled not at all. He looked somehow like a relative because of his features which, though they did not belong to any specific person she had known in other times, melted into a sort of human landscape she had once glimpsed, or had known instinctively. It was reemerging now from memory into consciousness. What was most noticeable in him was the melancholy in his glance, shielded by heavy, half-closed eyelids; it was his dark complexion, his rough manner immediately redeemed by his worried concern, and the anxious insistence of his questioning, which was contradicted by the fatalism of his conclusions. Because of that familiarity, she saw more clearly into the conflict that had followed her arrival. Ruben had not understood her sense of loss, nor her need to be loyal to Italy – the country that had rejected her but remained within her along with the familiar faces whose absence she was feeling on that spring day. Nor had he understood her way of defending her past in the only way she knew how: a way that was petty and fearful, ignorant of the generous daring of a revolutionary and unaware of the immense distance he had traveled through all of Europe – from Kiev to this last quiet refuge wedged between the Nazi army and the Atlantic. The history of her twenty years of life was domestic, made up of attachments and merits that she herself found empty and laughable at the very moment she resorted to mentioning them.

On the other hand, her discovery of Ruben's misfortunes and Spain's destruction wounded her conscience, but only as a delayed and useless reproach for a lack of action and an indifference that had not been hers alone. As a matter of fact, this reproach did not even properly apply to her because she was so young. Yet, since she had made her way out of Italy's complicitous silence, it was she who had to acknowledge and shoulder that monstrous and now unavoidable burden. Ruben, with his mocking manner, had wanted to make her understand that the persecution she was suffering at such a late date, and which she used to protect herself and play the victim, could never be confused, at least in his eyes, with political risks that had been deliberately and consciously taken. In other words, he had wanted to place a sort of distance between the freedom he had chosen and the choice she had made. She was a refugee, that was true, but late, by mistake, and in total comfort.

Still, his sarcasm had been tempered by the kindness and compassion that had infused every moment of their encounter and ultimately addressed his own nervousness as well as her vanity. That light sarcasm grew out of an ancient, unspoken familiarity that dated back to an equally ancient and never-forgotten pact of alliance.

And so, she was expecting to see him again – a foreign and familiar presence, forgotten and already on the verge of being remembered, an irritable and concerned man – as she walked up from the city back to Pensione Europa.

CHAPTER EIGHT

The Dining Room

She came face to face with him as soon as she entered the hotel; he was seated in one of the rattan café-style armchairs to the right of the porter's desk. He was not alone, and he was not the Ruben of the evening before, not Jean Gabin–like, with trench coat and felt hat worn low over his eyes. Wedged in the armchair that was too narrow for him, Ruben was wearing a dignified brown and white hound's-tooth suit. Reminiscent of a slightly absurd, bygone spring season, the suit, with its rather tight arms and shoulders, accentuated his thickset frame and his olive complexion, making him look now Middle-Eastern rather than French.

Grouped around him were several people whom the girl, at first, took to be hotel acquaintances. They seemed to be unrelated not only because of their ages and the way they presented themselves but mostly because of their way of being together. Seated facing Ruben was an old gentleman wearing a dark beret and holding a cane with an ivory handle; he was extremely pale, had a distinguished air, and stared down at the rug through the thick lenses of his glasses. Next to him, seated in another armchair, a plain-looking lady continued her knitting. She was not old; as a matter of fact she had no particularly distinguishing characteristics with the exception of a navy blue coat or coatdress with a white collar, like that of a governess or a nurse. And then, a bit farther, perhaps belonging to this same group too but turning her back to it and leaning with her chest and elbows on the reception desk, there was a third person, totally absorbed in a lively conversation with the young porter. Of this third person, the girl glimpsed, as she walked toward the group, only a big brown chignon above shoulders that were wrapped in a light-colored pullover, round hips, and a long, straight skirt. When the lady heard Ruben greet the girl, she turned around abruptly. And raising her head high, she extended her hand in an ample and generous movement. The gesture suited her tall body and especially the serenity of her classic features that her hair, parted in the middle, left entirely free, from her beautiful forehead to her straight nose and full lips.

"I am Elisabeth," she said simply.

That, then, was the name of Mrs. Ruben, while – according to Ruben's vague introductions – the gentleman's title was "Professor" and his name Schwarz. The plain woman in blue, who had no other titles, was left only with the perhaps inaccurate identification of "Mademoiselle Lebeau." After that, all five of them filed into the dining room, very slowly because the Professor walked leaning painfully on his cane and turned right and left greeting the other diners.

Not even in the dining room, at first, was the puzzle completely solved, because of the way the couples settled at two different tables, both placed in the recess of a large window overlooking the garden: Professor Schwarz and Mademoiselle on one side, the Rubens and the girl at the table near them. They might have just met, or become casually acquainted, and joined their lots by spontaneous impulse or simple accident in a proximity that left them free vis-à-vis each other.

The dining room was small and intimate. It was divided into alcoves by white columns with large capitals; some of the alcoves faced the wide windows but all of them were enclosed and private enough to contain two or three tables. Given the makeup of each family, the way the tables were placed, and the courtesy of the service, which was very concerned with etiquette, one was reminded of the atmosphere found in a family pensione of a resort area. Yet the silence that reigned there was too heavy, too melancholy, and the children, even the youngest ones, did not laugh or shout much. The large groups of diners at the far end of the room toward the big windows were extended families with children, parents, and also grandparents. You saw some men, worried, arrive late or leave in a rush, but there were others who lingered for a long time after the meal, silently smoking and drinking coffee.

"Oh," said Ruben, "those people are all waiting. Not at all like you. Visas, ships, papers. Toward North America or South America."

It didn't look like he was in the mood to offer further explanations.

"This is a sort of clinic. A waiting room. After a while, one just can't stand it anymore."

CHAPTER NINE

The Rubens and the Schwarzes

Through the large windows, one could see the big multicolored bushes tossing wildly, the hydrangeas, the hibiscus, the oleanders, the camellias in the little park, and even the tall umbrellas of the palm trees and the pines. "It's the wind from the Atlantic," said Elisabeth. It blew constantly in Lisbon, sometimes more and sometimes less, like the mistral, but perhaps it didn't cause headaches as badly. And then in February and April it became almost a hurricane. That's why all ocean crossings were hard during those months.

"It's better to wait to embark," she said with a vague smile that the girl did not know how to interpret.

From the upholstered interior the wind could not be heard. The effect was that of a curiously remote spectacle, like a film with no sound track. The city was far away, with its hum of moving crowds and streetcars, the noise from the port and the sirens' screams; the old quarter was barely visible through the trees, a blur of whitewash and red brick; the only background for the well-bred voices of the diners was a low, melancholy music.

To the girl's surprise the cuisine mixed different flavors; it was at the same time mild, sweet, and spicy. The delicate dishes began with the aroma of ginger and ended with a flavor of marzipan, leaving one in doubt as to what had really been tasted. The girl loved them, but the Rubens on the other hand were tired of them and ordered different dishes, describing at great length, with obstinacy and pique, all the cuisines they had experienced in all the places and restaurants, even the famous ones, where they had dined.

They said that the food was not well cooked, or that they had already had it the day before, even if prepared in a slightly different way, and they discussed at length whether or not it was a good idea to send it back.

"Really, they are exaggerating," Ruben would say in a gruff manner. "It's true that we do not have a choice, but we are not obliged to accept everything they force on us, either."

Elisabeth then would engage in long and complicated negotiations with the waiter, who was young and blushed timidly when confronted by her loquacity. Elisabeth, as a matter of fact, spoke Portuguese very fast, and if she did not know a word she would quickly replace it with another one in Spanish or French. Or she simply smiled the bright, candid smile that lit up her blue eyes.

"You have to assert yourself," she would explain to the girl. "Juan is right. They are taking advantage of the situation. And besides, they are primitive, medieval, stunned by all this tourism that has suddenly landed here. They are not bad, they just don't know how to manage this."

"On the other hand, as you have probably noticed, Elisabeth can manage quite well," said Ruben. "She never gets lost. No telling what she will do in America. But she is authoritarian; she is a Prussian."

"How silly." But Elisabeth seemed far from being annoyed and had certainly noticed, from the beginning of the meal, the girl's admiration for her. "Yes, I am German, but don't think that I pride myself on that. And really, do I look authoritarian?"

"Absolutely not," answered the girl with sincerity.

She had not known which nationality to assign to Elisabeth, and she had just wondered if Elisabeth too was Russian, or French, and in which one of his peregrinations Ruben had met her. In fact, when thinking of Elisabeth, all that had come to mind were those images, self-possessed, polished, and charming, that she had admired for years in the society magazines her English teacher had regularly lent her. The teacher used to say that to leaf through the *Illustrated London News* and the *Tatler* was in itself a good exercise. But really, for the girl, who did not understand the captions, the exercise consisted of becoming lost in contemplation of the debutantes, the young wives of lords, and even the baronets' fiancées. She became acquainted with them first in the photos of their betrothals and imminent nuptials, their portraits complete with necklaces and hairdos with symmetrical waves; then in their full-length portraits, with a fireplace in the background, when they were ready to be received at Court, wearing long dresses with trains, coronets, and diamond *rivières*; and finally, happily married, in family groups, with two or three angelic children in their short dresses and long pants, all artistically arrayed around their mothers, who sat quite straight on gilded armchairs. No less fascinating was the attempt to match those polished and evanescent characters with stories about betrothals and weddings, trying to imagine why in heaven a younger son had obtained a lady's hand or an "honorable" had wedded a simple "miss" whose mother, however, was a marchioness. Her conclusion was that there must have been something behind the scenes in those ceremonies, a background, some explanation. But for the girl, all that would forever remain a secret.

Elisabeth, who in this respect was also similar to the women in the *Tatler*, liked to go into details as if she had all the time in the world and as if it were important to establish all the facts with precision: what year they had attended the Odéon; where that famous restaurant that served only fish was located; why the cuisine in Zurich, although Swiss, was better than the cuisine in Basel, which was closer to France; and why, when in Rome, in spite of the warm insistence of their friends, she had always refused to eat at Alfredo's (it had to do – she said – with that gold tableware, which she found disgusting). She spoke about the events rather than about the time when they had happened, such that her past life resembled a plain filled with cities and houses and meals but devoid of the borders and valleys and mountains that would have marked changes and displacements.

Some of those trips or expeditions, which had served who knows what leisure pursuits or vacations or business affairs, must have included Juan also, or so the girl understood.

On other trips, however, Elisabeth had been alone, or in different company. At times, while speaking, Elisabeth turned her body slightly toward the table of their neighbors, the Schwarzes, as if she meant them to listen. In other instances, she did not turn at all and leaned toward Juan and the girl. And Juan always listened to her, smiling and adding some detail here and there. Not only did he not become irritated as he did in other moments – when he seemed constantly nervous and agitated, with his ear tuned to the telephone, ready to raise his head quickly whenever the porter or the doorman entered the dining room searching for someone – he actually looked pleased. Perhaps, thought the girl, Ruben drew courage from those tales about the past, a posthumous consolation, a sense of enduring wealth.

At the other table, which was behind the girl but at an angle, there was almost no talk. Silence reigned, interrupted only by some brief order imparted by Mademoiselle to the waiters. Mademoiselle had a courteous but toneless voice, and she pronounced with a very thick French accent a few Portuguese expressions and words that had to do only with the service and the food. She did not initiate any conversation with the Rubens. It was Elisabeth who would turn toward her and ask a few questions: if they had gone downtown, if they were going to go again in the afternoon, and how was her rheumatism. Minor questions, certainly, but the other woman answered them with precision and courtesy, without the hint of gaiety that Elisabeth put into every one of her gestures and words.

More than the well-bred and laconic voice of Mademoiselle, it was the obstinate silence of Schwarz, so much in contrast with the Rubens' bright and lively memories, that led the girl to think that there was, between the two couples, something other than an occasional friendship. Schwarz was deliberately silent, like someone who has already spoken at length and doesn't need to indulge in social chatter; or like someone who finds the conversation banal, or familiar, and does not deem it necessary to participate; or simply like someone who, tired and ill, finding himself in the midst of old friends, doesn't feel the need to make an effort. It could have been any of those things. Little by little, the girl realized that the silence at the other table was the same thing as a conversation, and the Rubens saw it as such. And yet, for some reason, it was against that silence that the Rubens felt the need to struggle.

CHAPTER TEN

Many Homelands

The girl watched the other couple for a long time, but with sideways glances, and noticed that the professor was intent upon eating: he had finished his little soup of vegetables in broth and was now bringing to his mouth the meat that Mademoiselle had already cut into pieces. It seemed that the operation worried him, and judging from the way his head was bent over the plate, one would have thought him blind, or at the least, very nearsighted.

It has been years now, Elisabeth was saying, that we have been living only out of suitcases and trunks: two trunks, eight suitcases. Can you imagine what it means to pack them up each time? And yet we are lucky, Juan said, if we have the chance to pack them. Sometimes our departures were so hasty that we had to leave everything behind. Just think, Elisabeth said, that when we returned to France after the war, after the Civil War that is, the first thing they asked us was *vos bagages*? They could not believe we had crossed the border with only the clothes on our backs, without anything else, Juan added. Elisabeth again took up the story: in Casablanca, she said with melancholy, we again loaded ourselves up with lots of possessions; in my room I cannot even turn around anymore, not that it is a bad room – actually, it is quite big for a hotel room – but aren't hotel rooms awful? Tiny pots for warming things, travel irons . . . well, it would be better not to buy anything and wait to buy in America. But we did not know, Mademoiselle Lebeau added from the other table. We could not have imagined that we would spend the whole winter here and also the spring. She was pouring a bit of white wine for the professor and continuing to make signs of assent and agreement with her head, thus making clear the fact that she too had participated in the last move. But you must understand, Ruben said – and he turned to the girl and certainly spoke only to her, as if there were no need to remind everyone else of their common misadventures – that from Paris, when the Germans arrived, we made a real escape. Who would ever have believed such a sudden downfall to be possible? Who would have guessed that Mussolini, the swine – and here his eyes shone with sarcasm, as if he had returned in his own mind to the discussions of the previous evening – that big swine of yours would stab France in the back? We closed the apartment in a wink, with everything inside, and we left. We abandoned everything, furniture, pictures (the ones we had saved from Germany), even a candelabra that I had brought from Russia – everything, all our memories. And those few things from Spain. From Spain? asked the girl. Oh yes, Ruben answered, we told you, we crossed the border in November, with the last refugees.

In my head it all gets confused, Elisabeth said. Seriously, there are days when I no longer understand a thing. I don't care about objects, in fact I feel lighter when I don't have anything with me. But it is the mental confusion that worries me. It's better not to think about it, Ruben advised. I no longer think about houses or landscapes or walls or trees I have seen. There is just one law: *c'est ici que je suis.* The girl, for the first time, felt ashamed that she had so little in life to forget.

That may be, Elisabeth said, but I go on looking for some object, and then I realize that I have left it who knows where. And really, there are some memories that have me obsessed. Ever since yesterday I keep seeing a samovar, all shiny, and a bearskin rug on the floor, and I am sure they must have been together, and yet I cannot place them: where were they, to which house did they belong?

"Heidelberg," Professor Schwarz said, all of a sudden. "To the house that looked out on the Neckar river, beneath Philosophers' Way. It was the green living room with the frescoes."

Elisabeth blushed, almost up to the beautiful brown of her hairline. Then she began quickly to speak again. The room is big, but I cannot stand seeing the same faces over and over, Elisabeth went on. The guests, the doorman, the elevator boy. At this point it is just a question of a little time, Ruben interjected. Most of the work is done. Yes, of course, Elisabeth nodded, yes, I agree, but by now it should be time to go.

The girl realized that the Rubens had been there, at that same table, for a long time.

"Ah, yes, four months," Juan said. "Yes, that is a lot, but

there is still so much to do. As long as there is time. In a little while it will be too late."

They had interrupted him by calling him to the telephone at various times; he would get up and run off, with that slightly heavy body of his, which was far from graceless, making his way quickly through the tables. "*Je vous demande mille fois pardon.*" Then he would throw himself behind the big desk of the hotel office, where the only public phone was to be found. His words could be heard all the way to the end of the dining room, excited words spoken in various languages: enthusiastic, warm, furious, or else depressed, but always enigmatic, and nothing more than mere allusions.

"They don't leave him in peace for a moment," Elisabeth sighed.

The girl asked: "Is he writing articles?"

Elisabeth, almost scandalized, stared at her: "What in the world would you have him write? Waiting to depart, in this situation that is so dangerous? Besides, you might say he doesn't even have a desk to write on. It has been months and months since he has written down even a single line."

So they had spent Christmas in Lisbon, and New Year's, the girl thought, and she went back in her mind to the winter that had just ended: to the waiting for the documents, to her mother's haste, and to the days that had slid by silently and rapidly like sand in an hourglass. She was still in Rome, she did not even know how she was going to manage to get all the way to Lisbon, and meanwhile the Rubens were already poised, so to speak, with their wings unfurled. But Easter had come and gone, and they had not yet departed.

"Last year we were in Paris during this season, the year before in a concentration camp in the south of France, and the year before that, Madrid had not yet fallen. Gabrielle has never spent two Christmases in the same place, nor an entire year in the same school. She has never been present at the close of the school year, she says, to receive any prizes."

"Who is Gabrielle?" the girl asked.

"Gabrielle? She is Juan's daughter. She is eleven, and she is a dear," Elisabeth answered.

"Oh," said the girl, "and where is she now?"

"Here," said Ruben, who had returned, and was looking around for the plate that the waiter had taken away. "Where can he be? That boy is an idiot. It doesn't matter, I shall eat the ice cream. Her mother left for the United States a month ago, but Gabrielle is listed on my passport and is staying here with me. She is at a boarding school with the nuns, right nearby, but she will not manage to finish the school year this time either."

"It is too complicated to keep a little girl in a hotel," Elisabeth wisely explained. "She would never be able to concentrate. And she is very gifted."

"She is the youngest in her class, you know," Ruben added. "And in one month she has caught up with the others. She is first in the class, perhaps even in the school. You must see the compositions she writes: she writes like a fifteen-year-old. And in Portuguese, no less. And she has never studied it."

"Gabrielle is very intelligent," the professor's voice suddenly added, and he was immediately echoed by Mademoiselle Lebeau: "Exceptional, I would say."

While they were speaking, it happened that the girl, instead of thinking about Gabrielle, thought about herself in relation to her dinner companions. In their lives she found elements that, at first glance, were not really very different from similar elements of her own life, or of that of her family or other families she had known till then; but they were laid out in such a way as to create a different pattern and impression, even an opposite one – just as on the reverse side of a carpet, the threads seem tied and woven in a simple way that reveals nothing of the imaginative colors and patterns visible only to those who see the correct side of the composition. The Rubens – and probably also the couple that she continued to call the Schwarzes (although with some uncertainty) – seemed to have enjoyed and exploited, without remorse, comfortable lives of ease and luxury even greater than her own. They had had houses, schools, trips to the most desirable neighborhoods and spots in Europe. They had been, and perhaps still were, rich and privileged, yet there was no way of applying to their lives the pattern of respectability that in the girl's upbringing and experience had always accompanied a stable and sedentary daily routine, dedicated to the solidity of life and to a secure future, and above all to the idea of a single religion and homeland. Just as they possessed friends and hotels and cities and schools scattered throughout the world, so too did the Rubens have at their disposal a plurality of homelands, and this bothered her. Instead of staying put like everyone else, and in particular like all of the rich and privileged people she had always known to be solidly attached to their

DIASPORA

houses, cars, or property, the Rubens went from east to west in slow migrations marked by hopes, battles, defeats, and continuous departures that had certainly cost them great effort but not great hesitation. Unlike the girl, who had been pulled away from Italy for the first time just two days before, her new friends were aristocrats of departures and nostalgias; they gave the impression of always being above those who had chased them and forced them to leave everything behind – whether they were Cossacks, Germans, Franco's troops, or even the Portuguese, whom the Rubens treated so haughtily.

The girl saw herself, in contrast to the Rubens, as fearful and clumsy, a sort of object in the hands of the enemy. The Rubens, instead, were fighters, always able to maneuver, to manipulate their weapons, to choose, if not salvation, then at least the method, place, and moment of their abandonments and flights. Flights that were really plunges into the future, which brought with it other escapes, other maneuvers, in a wide pattern destined to embrace their entire existence.

At this point she realized that the Rubens had again started to interrogate her. Questions about her life and her family in Italy, her relatives, friends, ancestry, and places of origin: the subjects, in other words, that at that very moment were occupying her mind. The tone of the questions, so much more friendly and discreet than those of the previous night, had put her off track, as did also the interruptions, quite frequent, that Elisabeth was making. She joined in often, in fact, sometimes outdoing her husband with that way of hers, of appearing at the same time to be both absent-minded and precise.

By going after details rather than facts, she would nevertheless finish by embracing, quite well and with great exactness, the facts themselves. The girl tended to answer Elisabeth rather than Juan. Elisabeth, as it turned out, had been, during some undefined period, in Italy and Rome, and was therefore able to clarify for Juan the girl's descriptions and explanations: her house, studies, schools, vacations, even her religious habits. Turned always toward Juan, and now totally disregarding the table of the Schwarzes, who had fallen back into silence, Elisabeth compared the facts of the girl's life with those of her own youth, her own journeys, convent schools, first communions, boarding schools, health spas in Middle Europe, all with a worldliness and a lightness that, with its irony, negated, at one and the same time, the importance of the questions themselves and of the answers.

After the last question and answer, Ruben spoke to his wife: "You see," he said, "I told you she could have been a Russian Jew."

Elisabeth quickly agreed, with a nod of her head, and the girl, for no reason, felt disturbed. They had judged her as if she had not been there, and above all, as if they were speaking only between themselves, in a private conspiracy that combined Elisabeth's gentle yet solid perspicacity with Ruben's wide experience of the world. And then, Ruben's observation had, in its brevity, the force of a judgment; after all the words the girl had used to create a flattering image of her past, it was as though Ruben had defined it as a false image, a fraud. It was a judgment that, to be frank, she could no longer manage to reject completely as she had done upon her arrival. On the other hand, that designation, "a Russian Jew," put her back into a tradition, into a category to which she was not sure she wanted to belong. And once again, there arose the problem of a single idea of nationality, of religion, of homeland – the problem that the Rubens had overcome with elegance, for themselves and for others, and that for her, on the contrary, was continuously present as an obstacle and a stumbling block.

At this point, brusquely, the luncheon ended. Ruben ran once more to the telephone, and since the Schwarzes seemed to have finished their meal some time ago – and a very frugal one, at that – Elisabeth motioned to the girl that she was ready to get up. From the hands of the young waiter, Elisabeth received a short fur jacket, which she threw over her shoulders and which, as it softly draped, wafted the fragrance of her perfume.

CHAPTER ELEVEN

Departures and Postponements

During the slow stroll toward the lobby, the girl happened to walk side by side with Mademoiselle Lebeau, and from close up she noticed how there was nothing remarkable about that face, with its regular features, the hair of a nondescript color, and the white skin already a bit wrinkled and lined around the eyes and the mouth. She was a pretty, refined woman, she had a pleasant voice, and she smiled with spontaneity; but compared to the other three people, she looked like the silent partner in a card game that requires four players. By contrast, Elisabeth's gestures were interesting and attracted attention even when seen from the back. During that brief move from one room to another, she helped the professor, bending toward him tenderly and in a protective manner, and holding him lightly by the elbow.

"Yes, that's true, he is leading a terrible life."

The girl had made a brief comment about the many phone calls that had interrupted Ruben's meal. She expected, at most, a nod of reply from Mademoiselle Lebeau. Mademoiselle, instead, interrupted her right away in a vibrant but low voice:

"Really, we don't know how long he can endure this and how long all this can last."

A blush had come to her face, usually white, and had made it look sorrowful without bringing life to it. The girl, sensing that she was making a mistake, said: "It will be a matter of a few days," and she thought of Juan and Elisabeth, their suitcases, the hotel room that was too confining, and their talks at the dinner table. However, Mademoiselle Lebeau added: "Who knows. He will leave, surely, I agree; we will leave, let's hope, surely. In the meantime, though, he keeps saying that doing this, doing what he does, is absolutely indispensable, and if *he* didn't do it, he who knows these problems so thoroughly, no one could or would want to do it. Besides, his collaborators have almost all gone; no one is left, really."

The girl realized then that Ruben's activities were a preoccupation even for Mademoiselle, therefore they were a shared preoccupation, and they all had a stake in them.

"We will stay till the end," added Mademoiselle Lebeau, and it was hard to understand if she was dissatisfied or resigned. "He says that we must wait. Wait, wait. But how will it all end? And what will the Americans decide in three, in four weeks? Where will the Nazi offensive be?"

Elisabeth had retraced her steps, in the meantime, after settling the professor and his cane on a rattan armchair. Now, sympathetic and understanding, she spoke as she had during the meal: "It's not fair to you, certainly. But you will see. In the end we always manage all right, don't we?" and she vaguely indicated the professor who was looking away in the distance. Mademoiselle silently nodded in assent, calmer now; and at that moment, as in a comedy, Ruben came back in.

He was very agitated and had a darkening face.

"So?" asked Elisabeth.

"So, nothing. The same. I have to run; there is a mass of people at the office."

"And what about the offensive in Greece, in North Africa? Any news from America, about Roosevelt's speech?"

Ruben was in a great hurry. "Oh, for the time being, things are going along, but we will have to see in a few days. That's all, I apologize, I must run. I don't know when I will be in touch with you tonight."

Elisabeth also seemed worried: "But it's Wednesday. Don't you remember? We promised Gabrielle that we would go get her this afternoon to take her out to dinner."

"Let's postpone it until tomorrow. I can't help it, there are more important things. I am leaving. Figure out something."

The girl stopped him with an energy that, given Ruben's humor, she felt was mad.

"Listen, I know that this is not the moment, but I should really tell you something else about my papers. I think that I am still missing a document. At the Jewish Community center in Rome they told me to get it here, I mean, in Lisbon."

Ruben did not show impatience but rather a vague politeness that clouded his eyes under eyelids immediately lowered.

"For this, too, I would say that we have time. Yes, I know, the boat leaves day after tomorrow. Fine, then we will talk about it tomorrow. Anyhow, it's late today and all the offices are closed. Why don't you go visit some place, go on a tour? Take a bus, a tourist bus that leaves from Rocío or from Commerce Square and go see the environs, Cintra, Estoril . . . you will see how beautiful Cabo da Roca is, marvelous."

CHAPTER TWELVE

The Edge of Europe

Outside, the girl found once more the acacias, the camellias, the hibiscus, the palms, and the graceful little angels with their harps, trembling in a leaden and sinister light that seemed to come from very far away. In the sky, against a layer that was already dark, big swollen clouds were galloping, constantly being replaced by other cloud formations that were driven on by the cruel and impetuous wind. The Atlantic wind that Elisabeth had mentioned had transformed the scene, until then static and almost serene, into an infernal saraband.

Down in the lower city too, the storm, although it blew less violently, had swept the tree-lined streets and the wide piazzas with their black and white mosaics, solemn porticoes, tall palaces, convents, and scores of equestrian statues. It had created a sort of time vacuum that only the storm could now fill. The bus, the only one that seemed headed toward the coast of which Ruben had spoken, was loaded with workers and local women who wore berets or black handkerchiefs on their heads. They were chattering loudly in a sweet and dramatic chirping, turning round every once in a while to smile at the girl, almost as if to excuse themselves for not sharing with her, as they would have liked to do, their tender intimacy.

It was a bit like her ride in the airplane: the girl found herself isolated once more, because she was younger and because she was wearing clothes that were too different and elegant. Besides, the whole expedition – due to the bad weather, the time of day, and above all, the way Ruben had pushed her to undertake it – was taking on the quality of a fated event she no longer was trying to escape, a quality that fit perfectly the lonely landscape toward which the bus was now moving.

At the onset, the landscape seemed similar to the one she had seen on arrival: after crossing the grandiose Lisbon of piazzas and churches, the suburbs appeared with their small houses and wide expanses of land, dotted here and there by structures and low factory buildings. After the camellias, the acacias, and the obelisks, a sort of sudden desolation appeared that not even the coming storm could free from its dust and poverty. The dust was rising up in little whirlwinds, and the ocean was hidden by wooden cabins eaten away by the wind and the salt.

Then, beyond the docks and the little houses and the fishermen's huts with their big stretched-out nets, the hotels, the palaces, and the grand-hotels made their by-now unexpected appearance, with high-sounding names that conjured up images of peace and repose: Miramar, Bella Vista, Astor, Excelsior, Europa, Peace and Crown, Queen, Victoria. From far away, in the gray light, not only were the avenues deserted, but the balustrades also appeared to be rusted, and the terraces, decorated by tall fixtures with white globe lights, seemed corroded by the dampness. The wide facades, all windows and balconies, and the entrances protected by porticoes, were blind and mute, barred up against a danger that to the girl seemed to go well beyond the elements, the sea-storms, the gales, and the winter season. She knew with certainty that the hotels would reopen within a few days; the big planks of wood that strengthened the great windows of the salons would disappear; and the empty terraces, now battered by the wind, would be filled once again with café tables and lounge chairs. And yet, despite this awareness, she found it impossible to imagine holidays, and carefree days, and relaxation in that strip of land hemmed in between a Europe abandoned to persecutors and victims and the ocean that hid submarines under its waves.

The girl turned her eyes to the coast: at times it was all tall cliffs and gorges, and the Atlantic beat against it with a crashing sound; but in other stretches it flattened into sand dunes, with tufts of yellow vegetation at the mercy of the storm. And the road at times stayed low, at times rose up; it disappeared between the forests of pine and eucalyptus. Then, down below, all of a sudden, howling among the rocks, the sea would return. When they had passed the last fishing village, there was a clap of thunder, like faraway cannon fire over all that gray, and then near, very near, prolonged and deafening. At the first rumbles, the chattering had ceased, only to start again, but softer. When the thundering became loud, over the sea that had suddenly calmed, the women made the sign of the cross, and some pulled out their rosaries. They began to pray, as loudly and intensely as they had previously gossiped, and no one spoke anymore. One woman, in fact, wanted to get down on the floor on her knees, but there wasn't enough space, and the bus continued to ascend.

They had forgotten the girl, who, on the contrary, now felt less isolated. It started to rain but without violence – a regular showering that drew a curtain over the beaches and the cliffs. From the coast now, there jutted out into the ocean the fantastic forms of enormous cliffs that the breakers covered and uncovered again. The leaden color of water and sky, of the very air humid and somber, made those cliffs into something different from the sea rocks and craggy peaks of milder seas and seasons. These rocks were black – eaten by the waves that penetrated deep inside them with foam, reflected light, and high sprays. And they were corroded by the ocean, even though they rose up like a bastion, as in obstinate resistance. At times, under the leaden sky, in the air that was now almost black, they merged with the Atlantic, sunken, invisible, gone – only to resurface again, no longer sea water but earth and rock.

A little man, who had changed seats and placed himself next to the girl, leaned toward the window of the bus and, making a lot of gestures, indicated that she should look out. At first, the girl, who was already looking straight toward the cliffs, did not understand where to direct her gaze. But the bus stopped, and she realized that everyone was looking in the same direction.

Out where the dark cliffs leaned well out into the sea, a lighthouse rose up, with a beam that shone in the falling darkness. The Atlantic threw itself against it, thundered and roared, but the rock rose up unafraid, stretching out even as the other cliffs remained behind, out where there was nothing but ocean.

"Cabo da Roca," said the little man, and the girl remembered Ruben's words, and finally, she understood.

It was the last sign of land, the edge of Europe.

That evening the girl was alone again, and had no one with whom to share all she had seen. Upon her return, she found that the Rubens were having supper out, as usual, while the Schwarzes, the doorman said, had also retired, as usual, to their room to eat a light meal.

CHAPTER THIRTEEN

Gabrielle

The following morning she wandered again through the city, recognizing by now places and vistas. A warm, humid wind was blowing across the clear sky, and the girl caught the fragrance of wisteria in the hot yet stormy air typical of those days. She also recognized the formations of clouds that arrived galloping from the ocean, the blinding whiteness of the palaces, and the sleepiness of enclosed gardens filled with flowering shrubs. That season, tender and ripe, was all intertwined with the presence of the small band of travelers living in the Pensione Europa, who were guided by Ruben's combative energy – which made her feel that somehow, in a part of Lisbon unknown to her, Ruben was fighting not only for them, but also for her and in a sense for everyone. Within a few hours, Ruben had been transformed for her into a symbol of battles that ended victoriously even though they might be temporarily lost; he was a symbol of vicissitudes that – even if only in the very long run – were brought to a good ending with elegance and skill. And so the girl rested in the thought that ever since she had met him at the airport the road had been smoothed for her. She ended up by convincing herself, with a sort of fatalistic languor, that in the matter of the missing document, if it was truly missing, all she had to do was trust herself to him.

When she returned to the pensione at noon, she found the Schwarzes sitting on one of the benches in its small park. The Professor had a blanket around his knees, and without his beret he exposed to the sun a white, fragile skull, with little hair and surfacing veins. Mademoiselle was sporting another one of her dresses for some imaginary spring, navy blue with white accessories, and newly waved hair of a violent red.

Both of them, compared to the previous day, were at the same time older and younger because between them was seated a young girl who was speaking with great ardor.

As she spoke, sitting sideways so that she leaned on the professor and turned her other shoulder lightly toward Mademoiselle, the little girl was tracing complicated swirls on the avenue's gravel with the tip of her brown bootie. Her high-pitched voice, punctuated by bursts of laughter, could be heard from midway up the ramp, and both her companions listened to her with great interest. Schwarz especially seemed to have come out of his shell of old age and unwellness. Behind his glasses his eyes sparkled, and the usual lines of bitterness had disappeared from around his mouth. With the hand that was free of his cane he patted softly the red jacket that Gabrielle had abandoned by him on the bench.

Gabrielle was wearing a light-colored pullover and a blue skirt, from which emerged her long legs, with white socks pulled tightly up to her knees, knees that were still thin, as they are in growing adolescents. When the girl arrived in front of Gabrielle, she was met by a face that did not go at all with the uniform, which was appropriate for a traditional, elegant boarding school. Gabrielle's blond hair, slightly curly and cut ear-length, her eyes of a very deep gray-blue, and her small, slightly snub nose, so like her father's, gave her the ambiguous expression of those angels in Renaissance paintings, who play music and seem either to be crying or perhaps laughing – one doesn't know which.

Right at that moment, she was bursting with glee because it was Thursday, vacation day, no school, and the afternoon stretched open before her. But one thing managed to cast a shadow across her day: the absence of her father, who was again detained elsewhere.

"He is so unpleasant, he is so annoying. I never see him."

"What are you saying?" Elisabeth wondered.

"Yes, I am always alone," her eyes darkened, and suddenly she looked almost old. "Besides, I was going to ask him a lot of things."

She resigned herself to asking all the other people: Elisabeth, who was worried that Gabrielle was not eating enough; Schwarz and Mademoiselle, who followed the conversation from their table; and even the young waiter, who was accustomed to seeing her on her vacation days and joking with her.

She asked for information on all kinds of things: if she could go to the movies and who was going to take her there because her classmates were all busy already and had all gone home; what day the dog show that she was crazy about was going to be held, and if in America she was going to be able to buy a dog; if she could have permission to read some books for grownups that the nuns kept under lock and key, whereas her father said they were masterpieces; and where could she buy a new pullover.

"But you have lots of them, and it's gotten warm now," Elisabeth remarked.

"I need one for the crossing; father says that on the Atlantic Ocean it's as cold as in the mountains."

"Well, the crossing! It will be summer by then," and Elisabeth shrugged her shoulders. "Your father would do well not to talk so much."

Gabrielle looked at her in a dignified manner: "I don't understand. Anyway, I do need that *petit maillot*."

She spoke rapidly and nervously, like Ruben, going from French to German to Portuguese, depending on whom she was addressing. But she also knew English, she said, because she was studying it at school. Her classmates barely knew one language, they were all daughters of merchants or Portuguese aristocrats, they went out with a chaperon until they were eighteen years old, and they were as ignorant as goats. As for her, she knew *five* languages, and she counted them in her head, and then checked them on her fingers; yes, they were five. She knew German since birth because her mother was German; now she was already in America. Did the girl know that they were also going to leave for *les États-Unis* within three weeks?

Elisabeth said: "In three weeks, or perhaps four, it's not certain."

"Four!" cried Gabrielle in despair. "But the Germans are arriving! And then, the third trimester is starting. You are not going to make me take the last semester here, too; this school is too stupid!"

"Gabrielle, please," said Elisabeth glancing around.

The young girl started again with her listing: she knew French because she had learned it in Paris, and Mademoiselle Lebeau had reviewed it with her in Casablanca, so she knew it almost as well as German; she knew Russian because it was her father's language, and they had fun speaking it together because no one understood them, not even Elisabeth and not even Dieder, who really was Professor Schwarz; Spanish she had learned because Elisabeth, returning from Spain, had taught her a little bit in jest; and as for Portuguese, well, Portuguese . . . *all* of them spoke Portuguese badly, even her mother and her mother's husband, who had stayed in Lisbon eight months, waiting to sail; even her father, who really was gifted at languages, such that no one could ever guess what country he was from. Not even her father had really learned to speak Portuguese; he managed, that's all. But she had, yes indeed. And she adored making fun of all of them, going into stores and making people believe that she was truly from Lisbon; she could have died laughing.

"What makes you die laughing?"

The voice came from the other end of the dining room, and it was Ruben's. Gabrielle jumped up from her seat and threw herself into his arms. They remained tightly embraced for a moment, in silence, their heads close. The girl had the impression that Ruben was looking at her from above Gabrielle's blond hair.

"You did not believe me when I told you at the airport that I had a daughter. She is unbearable, but she is my daughter."

"She is unbearable, and because of that she is your daughter," said Elisabeth laughing. "For the last two hours she has been pestering us with her problems."

"But I am right, papa. Don't you remember that you had promised you would stay with me today, and we would go to the movies? You are never free, Elisabeth is never free, everybody always has things to do, and I have to stay in that prison all week long."

"Listen," said Ruben. He placed his hand, a bit thick and dark, on her small white hand and looked into her eyes.

Gabrielle looked away and said only: "It always ends up this way."

The girl intervened:

"I have nothing to do, and I know so little of Lisbon. Couldn't I go out with Gabrielle?"

Gabrielle and Elisabeth said in unison: "That's marvelous! What a good idea."

Ruben, however, shook his head saying no: "I am sorry, I know, I am a spoil-sport. But I was about to tell you that there is something urgent that you must absolutely do this afternoon."

"The documents from the Jewish Community?" The girl thought: He has remembered, everything is all right.

"Yes, in a way." Ruben was speaking quickly, and seemed even slightly ill at ease. "Listen, there is a person here in Lisbon whom I know well; he is a friend of mine, he is British. He has been living here with his sister for years, and has been in Italy several times. Many times."

"Yes?" The girl was still waiting.

"He would like to see you. Today."

"See me? What for?"

"Just to talk." Ruben raised his shoulders. "Well, do you want to go see him or not?"

"Fine," said the girl. "But does it have to be right now?"

"Yes, right away. Here is the address. It's not far, fifteen minutes from here. You have to take a streetcar."

"All right," said the girl.

But it was not all right with her. She felt dismayed, as when she had arrived, because of this encounter, this unknown that she had to face. And besides, she also, like Gabrielle, like all the others, was under Ruben's orders; she was irritated with him and at the same time, because of the trust he had inspired in her, she was unable to disregard his orders.

CHAPTER FOURTEEN

An English Interior

Outside, still perplexed about the visit to the office of the Jewish Community, which Ruben seemed to want always to postpone, she reflected on the fact that she had not really understood: Ruben's friend did not have anything to do with those documents. The Englishman might even be simply one of those people who fall in love with Italy and are devoured for years by nostalgia. Her English teacher, for example, the one with the *Illustrated London News*, was a bit like that. She had gone home to England just a short time before the fall of France, at the last possible moment, precisely because she had not wanted to leave Rome, where she had lived for more than twenty years. And no one even knew if she had managed to arrive in England, given what had happened at Dunkerque and all the rest.

Perhaps Ruben's friend might be able to get a letter to the English teacher or obtain some news of her. So, feeling some comfort at this thought, the girl started toward the tram stop. Then her afternoon began to unfold, and she found that it went quite easily.

Having gotten off the tram, she found herself in a neighborhood of wide streets, tree-lined and filled with a total silence that seemed to stretch out toward infinity.

The houses were low, two or three stories high, white or made of gray stone. They had double windows with little columns, decorations of colored ceramic, and little towers, balconies, balustrades with small capitals, and grates that were twisted or curved. On the street side, only the garden gates could be seen, with tall spikes and bars of wrought iron, entwined – like the facades – with dark purple wisteria and the crimson red of the bougainvillea, and shielded by shining magnolias, palms, and pines; on the other side, the gardens led their lives.

At the address she had been given, just beyond the gate, a courtyard paved with big stones opened up; between the stones, the first grass of spring was sprouting, and, in the middle, water spurted up in a fountain made of light blue majolica. All around, rose bushes, small trees, shrubs, and arbors hid the two low buildings that closed the patio at the other end. According to the instructions she had received, the girl directed her steps toward the small house on the left, with a door painted green and a knocker in the shape of a lion's head with the name clearly inscribed: Miss Gertrude Bell.

But the door was opened by a man with a pipe in his mouth. He removed the pipe right away, begging the girl's pardon:

"I was not expecting you so soon. This is so kind of you. Come right in."

The man was so British – with his salt-and-pepper hair and mustache, his thick and slightly worn tweed jacket –

and he blended so completely with the interior of the house, that the girl's resentment and even her worry disappeared completely. She was no longer displeased at having obeyed the rather incomprehensible order Ruben had given her. For in the comfortable and almost too cluttered living room, in front of the easy chair covered with chintz, with the curtains that hid the patio and the roses, and the flame in the fireplace that heightened the already strong fragrance of the daffodils and hyacinths in the vases, there again opened up before her, as if by miracle, the small universe, correct and orderly, of her English teacher.

"But this is England," she said impulsively, in Italian. "Oh, yes, at least a little slice of England," answered the man in Italian. "Do you know England well?"

The girl shook her head.

"No, not at all. I was supposed to go there, however; in fact, my English teacher had everything organized, but then the war broke out."

"Of course," the man observed. "What a shame." He made another pause. "Perhaps near the fire you will be too warm. You know how we English do not like the cold. What was your teacher's name?"

It came naturally to the girl to tell him the name and all the rest: that the teacher had left Italy almost a year ago, that her students were so afraid that she would be interned, and that they had finally convinced her to leave Rome. The girl also told about the lessons, the English newspapers she was given to read, and about the cold mornings, in winter, when the teacher walked up from the Spanish Steps and crossed on foot the park of Villa Borghese to get to her classes. She always took an ice-cold shower before going out; she was a Christian Scientist. She used to say that the Italians loved neither nature nor animals; and she considered every question according to the principles of fairness. "It's fair, it's not fair," she would say.

The man would nod every once in a while in agreement.

When the girl spoke of the material restrictions that were still tolerable in Italy, the Englishman neither asked her questions nor showed surprise. When she recalled the students who, two months earlier, had been called up by the army under the fiction of "volunteering," he did not ask her about their possible destinations. It was the girl who told what little she knew: an ensign had been injured on a ship still in port in Naples during an air raid; a cadet had been sent to Yugoslavia; a member of the Alpine Corps was fighting on the Greek front. She said: "All I have are military addresses in my address book. If they can be of any use to you, I will gladly give them to you. This friend of mine in the Alpine Corps has been in Albania since February. When I left Italy, his family had not had news of him for some time. I think he is in a very dangerous place, with ice and trenches and the Greek artillery just a few steps away."

The Englishman said, "What a shame. How sad. Destroy all the addresses before you embark. I think I know where your friend is. Recently, there has been a major Greek offensive. But your friend, I'm certain, must have made it through. Unfortunately, it will not end here: the Germans will intervene. They cannot allow their Italian allies to be thrown into the sea."

A silence fell. The fire crackled. From deep in the house, beyond the closed door, noises came to life, footsteps and creakings, muffled signs of existence.

The man rose to stir the coals in the fire, and with the bellows in his hand, half turned toward the girl, he asked, "And the *Ara Pacis*? The 'Altar of Peace'? How have they finally decided to protect it?"

The girl thought for a minute. "Yes, I remember now, I passed by it just a few days ago. It seems to me that they have replaced the large glass enclosure with big wooden planks. To protect it against the bombs."

"Of course," said the Englishman. "That is good. It is so beautiful. It would be terrible if something happened to it."

A lady entered with a tray and silver service for tea. She was tall, of middle age, with all-white hair and violet eyes.

"Today is our maid's day off. The Portuguese hardly give any freedom at all to their servants: everyone is off to mass on Sundays, and that is all. It is not fair."

"It's true," said the girl.

The tea was aromatic, the scones smelled like sugar candy, and the bitter-orange marmalade came from Scotland.

The woman poured the tea ever so slowly and made, just as slowly, the decorous observations of the teatime rituals.

"Do you take milk? Do you take sugar? We have been here for twenty years. Yes, that is a long time. No, I would never move. At this point, it's home. But we go back to England every summer. No, not this summer. Oh, yes, Ruben is a darling man. Have you also met the Schwarzes?"

The sun, still high, was now shining aslant into the room, illuminating the Empire clock over the fireplace, the numerous family portraits standing on the round table with the padded tablecloth, the slightly overblown roses on the chintz fabric, the newspaper racks, and the flowering branches in the tall vases.

"One must have a permanent place," said the woman. "If not, when the storms come, the difficult moments, what can one do? Yes, this is a beautiful house, we are very fond of it."

The girl asked suddenly:

"Monsieur Ruben is extraordinary, wouldn't you say?"

The Englishman answered after careful consideration: "I believe he has saved more people, more children, more fugitives, more Jews, than anyone could ever imagine."

"And if the Nazis were to arrive even here?"

"In France there is already a great price on his head."

"A bit more tea?" asked the woman.

"And Professor Schwarz is so old and run down. Will he manage to leave for America?"

The Englishman, leaning on the fireplace, changed position and began again to puff on his pipe:

"Schwarz is a strong man. He is very famous, you know, as a philosopher. Now he is just a shadow of what he once was, but you should have seen him in the old days, how spirited and pleasant he was."

"And Mrs. Ruben?" the girl insisted.

"Here is the sugar for you," answered the woman. "Elisabeth has always been the same. The incarnation of beauty, the one with whom everyone falls in love."

CHAPTER FIFTEEN

Balalaika

On her way out, the girl opened the patio gate and then closed it carefully, leaving behind her, after a last glance, the green door, the rose bushes, the tender grass, and the fountain that chattered in the quiet of the afternoon. Once on the road, she breathed in deeply the fragrance of wisteria and acacias with the slight hint of salty air that she had come to recognize. It was still very early for the city to come to life, and silence reigned on the wide streets that seemed to have no end.

She found Gabrielle and Elisabeth in the dark and deserted lobby. Only one lamp lighted the head of the porter who, crouched behind the desk, was absorbed in his crosswords. Gabrielle, in her restlessness, was making a last attempt to convince Elisabeth to go with her to the movies.

"There is still time before dinner. Couldn't the two of us go?" the girl suggested.

Both jumped at the offer with enthusiasm. Gabrielle, in her haste, could not even find the sleeves of her red blazer.

"*Balalaika*, please – not *Snow White*."

"Certainly," Elisabeth immediately agreed. "They are so boring, those dwarfs."

Since the show was to begin in only a few minutes, they almost ran, and Gabrielle, who knew all the little streets and alleys between the tall buildings, pulled the girl by the hand. At the movie theater they settled into comfortable seats, having had just enough time to provision themselves with candy. The film was dubbed in Portuguese, and the girl, who felt a bit tired, would perhaps have closed her eyes once in a while, if Gabrielle had not been there ready to translate at great speed from beginning to end, afraid that the girl might miss even one word.

Gabrielle sat a bit hunched forward, her elbows resting on her knees, almost at the edge of her seat, and at certain points she even bit her nails out of fear and emotion. When she realized it, though, she would say: "Oh, papa doesn't want me to." She would then take another candy, settling way back, leaning on the back of the seat and crossing her legs. Occasionally she would turn a radiant face toward the girl and ask, "Do you like it? Isn't it wonderful? I am so glad we didn't have to go see *Snow White*."

At the film's comical or light moments, which were rather rare, she laughed out loud with gusto, so noisily that the dignified Portuguese turned around. But the dramatic scenes, the protagonist's flight, the parting of the two lovers, and the insistent, obsessive, and dramatic sound of the balalaika transformed her fine aristocratic profile into a hard mask, almost that of an old person. Looking furtively at the bitter grimace of her mouth and her misty eyes, the girl saw an image of Gabrielle that was completely different: a Jewish little girl, as she was, Hungarian, or Polish, or Russian, caught up in a dramatic destiny.

But Gabrielle would change right away and would say, "It's fantastic, isn't it? I love sad stories so much."

At the end of the show she dried her eyes.

"It was marvelous. I will never forget this afternoon," she said, adding that with Elisabeth she would not have had even half as much fun.

So, they started walking back up the avenues, very slowly, stopping in front of the lighted store windows. Gabrielle, hanging on the girl's arm, kept chattering like a magpie. She explained that the merchandise seemed beautiful, at least when compared to that in Casablanca or in Paris, where by now there were Nazis, and no one wanted to buy anything any more; but actually it was really awful, in the Portuguese taste, and Elisabeth said that one might as well wait until New York with Fifth Avenue and Park Avenue, which had marvelous stores and the pullovers especially were magnificent.

"I can't wait to get there, to New York," Gabrielle said "and my God, what a bore going to school tomorrow morning. At times like this *j'ai toujours le cafard*; I always feel depressed."

The girl, just to say something, interjected, "But you are so good at school, you are first in your class."

That was true, said Gabrielle, but she was also the youngest and perhaps because of that she was depressed.

"They always talk among themselves," she added, "they have so many secrets, and they say that they can't tell me because I can't understand anyhow."

The girl felt that she had no consolation to offer.

"You, too, will grow up," she said just to say something, to give her an answer.

"Sure, but that doesn't matter. I'll leave, and so they won't tell me anything anymore."

They had reached the ramps and were ready to go up.

"What about you, when will you arrive in America?" Gabrielle asked suddenly.

"In eleven days. I mean, if all goes well. And you in about a month."

"Yes," said Gabrielle, "more or less. But you know, our papers are not at all completely in order," she said judiciously. "Elisabeth's last name is still Schwarz, and her passport is with Dieder, who used to be her husband, but now papa is. But they got married in Spain during the war, so how can you prove it! And the Americans are very fussy about adultery, and it could happen that when we arrive they will stop us and quarantine us, but papa says that in the end they will have to let us disembark, and then we will be settled forever."

"Of course," said the girl, and she looked around her.

A great silence had fallen over the city and the lights on the esplanade shone, just above the ramp.

"Gabrielle, we must hurry, it's very late."

They took each other's hand again and started climbing the stairs two by two. This is the Diaspora, the girl thought to herself. And she saw the city, all dotted with lights, slip by her, on the other side of the balustrade, as she had seen the green fields of Europe slip away from her, under the wings of the airplane. Tomorrow evening, on the ocean, these lights will be no more, she thought. This is, for all, the moment of the lights' dimming, the loss of all love and safety. All end in the Diaspora. We must all show papers and credentials, to prove who we are and who we were. Even the leaders, even the strong ones, even those whose task it is to guide and save the others, even the infallible ones, like Ruben. Even he, he who is the infallible and noble patriarch, he who makes the noble choices, he now – with cunning and subterfuge – has to take himself and his little tormented and tightly bound clan into safety.

"What's the matter?" asked Gabrielle. "Don't worry if we are late, papa will certainly not get angry with you."

They were at the top now, and suddenly the girl spied Ruben on the doorstep of the Pensione Europa, between the two large globes at the entrance, silhouetted against the light coming from the inside.

He opened his arms to receive them, and they went in that way, all three together, he in the middle holding one on either side.

"Good girls, you came back," he said, and Gabrielle and the girl both looked at him in astonishment.

"We went to see *Balalaika*; it was fantastic," Gabrielle announced with great emotion.

"I received news about your visit," said Ruben addressing the girl. "I am really pleased."

CHAPTER SIXTEEN

A Birthday

In that in-between hour that preceded the aperitif for the Portuguese and followed the guests' dinner, there were, again, very few people. From the semideserted bar came distinctly the usual musical medley.

"Everything is fine. Mr. Bell is most impressed with you."

The girl was still thinking how Ruben had shown her a Europe that was unknown to her, borders crossed with poise and nonchalance, just on the strength of the nobility of his feelings and ideas.

But now he must have returned from a difficult day, because his voice sounded veiled, subdued rather than tired. His suit also, too light in color for the hour of the day and the season, seemed tight in the shoulders, and the lines on his brown face were dark and deep. That was why the girl did not understand, at first, what he was talking about; by now, she saw him tossed in the storm like she was. Even worse than she was, because he was helping everybody else, but his documents were not in order. His papers were missing, or they were actually false, at least from the point of view of the authorities he would have to face in the United States, those who would come on board the ship and who would have to be made to understand, somehow, the relationship among the four of them. As far as it concerned Europe, or himself, or the battles he had fought, it didn't matter how they were related, the two, the four, or the five of them, including Gabrielle. But in the American paradise that he had to enter at all costs, it mattered indeed. The plutodemocratic Jew, Ruben, with the many names and cultures and his one personality, was going to be forced to assume a definitive name. If he could succeed in doing so.

"Do you hear me?" asked Ruben. "You look tired. Perhaps you did too much. But it was worth it; now everything is set. Tomorrow morning you can go by the British consulate, you will find Mr. Bell there, they will give you your *navicert*, and everything will be ready to go."

"The *navicert*? Mr. Bell?" the girl still did not understand; she still believed that Ruben had been the bulwark between her, such as she was at her arrival, and Lisbon and the world. She had thought him invincible and invulnerable, but now who was she going to find to protect her?

Ruben started to laugh, a bit tiredly.

"But you had not understood at all then? You are not going to imagine that I sent you on a social visit. Bell absolutely *had* to see you."

The girl understood, then, and she was truly frightened. It was not only the Ruben family that had changed, in that half hour, but she also had changed. Everything that had happened since her arrival had been a sham. There had been no friendship and no concern but only vigilance, and their questions had all been asked with a purpose.

She said, "But . . . you did not trust me, did you?" in a tone that sounded arrogant to her; yet she actually knew that she was frightened, inside, not so much because of what had happened, but how she had been subjected to judgment during those days and observed like a stranger.

The situation had turned around in just a few minutes: the Rubens were defenseless, but a word from them could have kept her forever in Lisbon, with Italy and America equally inaccessible.

Elisabeth, who arrived on the scene at that moment, interjected right away, with embarrassment, "Not at all, dear, that's not it."

Ruben said softly, "Are we ready to go to have dinner or not?"

All four swiftly filed into the dining room. Gabrielle, blushing and with darkened eyes, looked at their faces, one after the other.

The dining room was deserted, as if nothing were to happen there any more and not even morning would ever arrive again. Empty, without plates or silverware, was the white tablecloth on the Schwarzes' table. A few guests were ending their dinner at the other end of the room, beyond a zone of silence and darkness.

The Rubens, the girl, and Gabrielle also remained silent a moment, and the girl thought that perhaps there was never again going to be a way to communicate and to start once again to know each other.

"Wait," said Ruben, and he hastily gave the orders to the

waiter who, tired and listless, had approached the table. "I am going to explain."

Ruben's face was still drawn; the deep lines that in such a dark complexion now marked tiredness would before long mark the coming of old age.

She felt compassion, but still she said, "What is there to explain?" in a petulant tone that reminded her of their first encounter and her arrival. She had felt insecure and irritated then because everything seemed to be slipping away, or changing meaning, and above all because there was no sure hold on things.

Now, she was losing her sense of self, that self that in the Rubens' eyes, for three days, had represented something different from what she meant to convey, and from what she believed she was and had been all her life. It was a self subjected to judgment, weighed, which now perhaps – because of something the Rubens might never view as an error – could be refused and rejected. So that once again, as in the case of Italy, and Europe, and her own family, she found it impossible to hold onto a sure support that she had been taught to trust.

"I am going to tell you now. I have only reasons for congratulations and celebration, and I find that everything is rather obvious." As a matter of fact, Ruben's face was becoming smoother now and relaxing, as if he were amused but not surprised by the girl's reactions. "You are very naive. You will learn. Don't you know that we must check all those who come through Portugal on their way to America and that the ship you will be sailing on tomorrow, God willing, will be filled to the rim with the scum from half of Europe – agents, spies, traitors? That the United States is not at war yet, and God only knows if it will ever go to war? And what about the Bund, what about America First, what about the fascist organizations that infiltrate the mass of refugees and use them to get information? Have you ever heard about them? Have you ever seen refugees, have you? Where have you been until now?"

"I know all about those things," replied the girl, offended. "And I know refugees." Yet, while she was speaking, she saw again in her mind the Jews from other countries who had arrived in Italy in previous years, little by little. To be truthful, they had not touched the life of the girl or that of her family very much. Occasionally, some of the refugees became students with fixed incomes, and that did away with the tragic aura of poverty and persecution that hovered around them. But those were few. The others, those whom the girl had seen in the last two or three years, had appeared unexpectedly from a sort of limbo unknown to her. They would arrive at bourgeois and still well-to-do homes usually at mealtimes, and send their appeals through the maid: "Dear Sir!" they would write in their ornate and almost gothic hand that clashed with the cheap sheet of paper, folded in two and lined. "My dear Sir! I address your kindness and generosity to obtain a little help. I am a German Jew (or Lithuanian, or Hungarian, or Viennese). I have lost everything, I must leave Italy, my wife is ill, and we will be expelled in a few days."

"Why accuse me?" added the girl. "I am Jewish; what side did you expect me to be on?" But she recalled that they, those refugees who had landed in Italy, had not even been evaluated but had simply been rejected or sent away, in great haste, because they did not belong to a familiar world, and there was no measure by which to judge them.

The appeals of those foreign Jews opened a wedge of malaise in the family meal since they brought along, beside dangerous specters, a bad conscience that it was not easy to assuage. The little help given did not serve any purpose, neither for the one giving it nor for the one receiving it. The receivers, after entering again for a moment the atmosphere of tranquillity that had once also been theirs, were swallowed up again by the city to which they had not even had the time to belong. The guests with frizzy hair and pale blue eyes had become more numerous for a while, in a sort of frenzy, then they had become sparse, and – just a few months earlier – had completely disappeared.

Ruben shook his head. "We have made so many mistakes, and for so many years! And precisely because we did not have the perspicacity to control. You are one of the last people, in all probability, to leave Italy and perhaps Europe. Do you realize that?"

"I know," said the girl humbly.

"And are you aware, are you, of the millions you are leaving in danger, behind you?"

"Please," said the girl.

"I beg you," said Elisabeth.

"What would have prevented the Fascist regime from using you for some objective? To show that the Italian Jews are not in such bad shape, to defuse a bit the antifascist propaganda, and foster good will in America?"

"Me?" The idea seemed absurd to the girl, who added suddenly. "But I told you only what I knew; I even told you all that I knew."

Ruben started laughing. "All that you told us we knew already. Mr. Bell knows Rome much better than you do – you must have understood at least that."

The girl could not resign herself. "But why haven't you understood who I was?"

Ruben looked at her. "But perhaps, you know, we *did* understand," he said.

Elisabeth said, "All right, now there is a surprise."

"Oh, yes." Ruben was really pleased with himself. "Our intelligence service has discovered something. And don't go saying that we are not efficient now. You turn twenty today. Is it true or not?" Then he looked at her: "And do not become emotional, I beg of you, because the champagne has arrived."

CHAPTER SEVENTEEN

New York, New York

It was as if the scene had been changed in a flash – by order, it truly seemed, of Ruben himself. From the bar next to the lobby, where all the lights had been turned on, the wide and sonorous waves of "La Belle Hélène," the feverish melodies of "La Vie Parisienne," and the enchanted rhythms of "Granada" suddenly came pouring out of a loudspeaker and over their heads. It was then that the girl saw the marvelous couple become frivolous and mellow, worldly and light-hearted, as generous and happy-go-lucky as they had once been in happier days. They bubbled with joy: elegant and warm, sophisticated and gay, they were projecting onto the coming years a past that seemed free of remorse or melancholy. They were inventing a future that was still possible, a future made of security, love, and friendship. With easy elegance, they were recreating the wide, open, rich world in which they had always wanted to live.

"We'll all get together in New York, right, papa? And we'll go see *Balalaika* again? You have no idea how good it was."

"Of course," Ruben said, "and many other films. We have an endless number of things to do."

"You know, when we were in Casablanca," added Elisabeth, "we used to console ourselves by making lists of the films we planned to see in New York, to make up for everything that was happening to us back then."

"We shall spend our lives at the movies," Ruben said. "But I will have to work a bit, if we are to eke out a living. Sometimes I cannot even remember in which language I will have to write – assuming, of course, that I have the time to write."

"Which language is your first language?" asked the girl.

"I only know how to count in Russian. That is about all I can say. Perhaps I shall die speaking Russian."

"We will finally have a house again," Elisabeth said, "a real house, with books and a study. I want a house in Greenwich Village. Everyone says it is so beautiful."

"Not me," said Gabrielle. "I want a tiny little house in the country. And a dog. A cocker spaniel."

"But there aren't any tiny houses, Gabrielle," said Elisabeth. "There are only those horrible suburban houses that stand all in a row. Would you want to live out there, where everyone does what everyone *else* does?"

"All right," Gabrielle answered with a generous impulse. "You can live in your skyscraper, and I'll stay for a while in the country and a while in the city."

"What about school?" Ruben asked.

"Oh, I'll finish in three or four years, and then I'll get married."

"Heavens! I was married at seventeen!" said Elisabeth.

"I would not get fixated on such matters, if I were you," Ruben advised them. "As for me, I shall be happy just to arrive and make a new start. And later, perhaps, to return."

The French melodies coming from the loudspeaker yielded to a habanera, then to a fandango. Ruben could resist no longer, so he took Gabrielle by the hand and they went into a *paso doble.* Moving their feet with small, rhythmic steps, they danced with serious countenances, standing a bit apart and staring into each other's eyes. Gabrielle was like a feather, and even Ruben's heavy body seemed to have become lighter and more refined, as though it had been touched by a gentle gracefulness.

"Look how solemn they are. They could almost be two Spaniards." Elisabeth observed. "Or two Russians."

Once they realized that the waiter was already half asleep and leaning against the wall, they took pity on him and rose to leave. But still they were strangely cheerful, and the few people present in the lobby watched with surprise as all four of them emerged arm in arm from the dining room.

The girl said, "Back home they'll have thought that I spent my birthday all alone. They don't even know that this has been the most beautiful night of my life. How can I ever thank you?"

"Oh, that is easy," Ruben said. "Just promise to spend all your birthdays with us. And promise always to be twenty years old, just as we all are tonight."

As she gave Gabrielle a goodnight hug, the girl felt with her hands the thin shoulders and soft curly hair of Ruben's daughter.

"Now remember our date in New York."

"When?" asked Gabrielle.

Ruben gave the answer. "I would say within two months at the most."

"Okay," said Gabrielle. And heavy with sleep, she climbed the stairs with Elisabeth, who held her close.

Ruben stopped in order to explain to the girl where she was to go the following morning, and what she was to ask.

"So then, everything is all set?"

"Of course," said the girl with a smile.

Then Ruben and the girl also started up. He went all the way to her room, and they entered together. Looking around, he observed with curiosity the objects that filled the room: her bags, her clothes on the chair, the brushes, the photographs. It was time to say goodnight. He took her by the shoulders and gave her a deep kiss. He caressed her, touching even her breasts, the back of her neck, and under her hair. His hands were confident. But the lasting impression, the one that stayed with the girl, was that of his mouth. Strong and fleshy, it held her; it searched and pulled, as if to draw something out of her and also communicate something important.

The girl stirred and tried to pull away. Almost immediately, Ruben let her go, but remained close, looking at her.

"I . . . don't know," the girl began to say. But Ruben motioned to her not to speak. He caressed her lightly on the cheek with the back of his hand, eyeing her with his usual gaze, half affectionate and half ironical.

"You will learn," was the last thing the man said. Then he opened the door.

CHAPTER EIGHTEEN

Navicert

The following morning, at the office of the Jewish Community, the girl found the waiting room full of familiar faces. They were men and women who were chatting amongst themselves timidly, in low voices, or else they were reading the newspaper. She had long been familiar with them, and had seen them quite often, especially the men, with their suits that were too tight at the shoulder, their jackets that were too short and even a bit faded. Their faces wore intense expressions, with deep wrinkles on the forehead, often with hair a bit curly and brushed back. Their faces had uncertain expressions even when their features were pronounced; their eyes were a bit watery and tired.

When the girl entered the hall, all the faces turned toward her, and the voices stopped. For a moment she wished she had not been wearing such a new gray wool suit, but then she realized that the destiny foretold by all the messages had arrived, a new solidarity had been established, and the only difference that existed now was between those who were going to leave and those who would stay behind.

"This is your *navicert*," Mr. Bell had told her at the English consulate. Behind the desk, he had assumed an official air that made one forget about the little green door and the chintz with the roses.

"And without this?" asked the girl.

"Oh, simple. You would have been stopped at Bermuda, made to disembark, and placed in confinement. Good luck."

The ship was to leave at five, and boarding was scheduled for three o'clock. At two, after she had said goodbye to Elisabeth and to the couple she continued to call the Schwarzes, the girl convinced herself that Ruben would not return in time to see her off. Elisabeth, on the other hand, was confident.

"He always arrives," she said.

Indeed, while the suitcases were standing in front of the door of the pensione, Ruben arrived in a taxi, opened the window, and announced, "Get in. We are going to the harbor."

So, they once more made a trip together, with Ruben pointing out the monuments of Lisbon just as if her stay, instead of ending, were about to begin.

Ruben was again dressed à la Jean Gabin, in a trench coat with the collar turned up; but the felt hat was missing because the spring weather had by now exploded with a vengeance.

"It seems impossible that only three days have passed," said the girl, "and I am so sorry to be leaving."

"When you pass it, do not look at Cabo da Roca," Ruben advised her with a smile, "and think only about your arrival."

Then he rested his hand upon hers, and held it all the way to the harbor.

CHAPTER NINETEEN

"Vive les États-Unis!"

The sun shone, still blinding, over the ocean, and on the quay there was great confusion. Make sure, Ruben had said, that you do not talk too much and do not mention names because at sailings there are always people who watch and observe. Anyway, the girl did not feel like talking about anything any more, and she would have preferred for Ruben not to waste any more time and leave. But Ruben said no, that she should not worry because he was enjoying staying there. It was true, a great animation reigned; and rather than a sailing, it looked like a sort of fair, with people shouting and singing and vendors selling balloons, souvenirs, blankets, and even deck chairs.

Ruben absolutely insisted on giving her a deck chair as a present.

"It's an investment," he said. "You can carry it on the bridge, and you won't need to rent one. And you won't make a dent in your five hundred dollars."

The girl could not dissuade him, so they embraced in the midst of all the people who pushed or cried or sang. The girl again had both hands occupied, with her big handbag on one side and on the other side a red and white deck chair.

Once she had boarded, she recognized some of the people

she had seen at the Jewish Community office earlier that morning; they now waved their hands and shouted without saying goodbye to anyone in particular.

And in the midst of all those voices, among the crowd that shouted "Long live Portugal!" "Long live America!" she was glad that Ruben was still there, on the quay, smiling at her with a slightly pensive air. Occasionally he would throw around an inquisitive glance and become meditative; then he would stir and smile at her again, and he would shout looking at her: "*À New York, aux États-Unis!*"

After playing the American anthem, the ship moved away from the quay. It was a slow and solemn departure that left her enough time to see Ruben, who had pulled out of his breast pocket a white handkerchief and waved it with one hand, while with the other hand, joining index finger and thumb, he made the gesture of perfect success, and shouted "*Vive les États-Unis!*"

Then she remembered his advice, and she went down to the lounge so as not to see Europe any more.

CHAPTER TWENTY

Exit

Five or six weeks after her arrival in America, the girl began to look for news of the Rubens and the Schwarzes. And, as Juan had foretold, she received a brief postcard from New York in the middle of June: everything had gone well, it said, and they had departed three weeks, more or less, after she had, on a cargo ship, and had arrived safe and sound. Now they were house hunting and trying to set things up, but they would write again soon and would get in touch to arrange their next meeting – that famous reunion, in fact, that they had planned for in Lisbon.

All during the summer, there were various exchanges of news: the Rubens were well, New York was stifling, but thank heavens, the war was going better, England was holding up, Germany had invaded Russia, and it was anyone's guess but perhaps this was the beginning of the end.

Since the girl did not live very close to New York and the Rubens had so much to do, their various plans to visit, despite all good will, had come to nothing; and the autumn came and still they had not seen each other.

The Bells also wrote from Lisbon. They sent their greetings and best wishes for the friends they had in common, and it seemed that for them, in the little house with the roses, life had not changed at all.

In the fall, the girl found out that Gabrielle had been enrolled at the French school, that the Schwarzes too were in New York, that the Rubens now had a beautiful apartment, spacious and picturesque, and that Juan, finally, had a study in which to write. She expected, every day, to see his name appear in the newspapers, to see his political opinions cited and his role in Europe discussed, but no matter how often she leafed through not only the daily papers but also the weeklies, she never saw anything and never read an article by him.

Before Christmas, the Rubens sent a greeting card from Juan, Elisabeth, and Gabrielle; the girl answered and also sent greetings to the Bells in Lisbon. Because she had suggested to the Rubens a specific date at the beginning of January on which to meet in New York, she was very surprised when she did not receive an answer.

It was already February when, via Switzerland, a note that had been opened and resealed by various censors arrived from Miss Gertrude Bell. She spoke neither of Christmas nor of anything else but only of the Rubens. It had been a terrible tragedy, she said, and she was certain that the girl was just as stunned as she and her brother had been. No one really understood why Gabrielle, right after Christmas, had suddenly thrown herself from the third floor, from the apartment where Juan and Elisabeth lived. Perhaps she had been unhappy at school, perhaps she did not like America; who could say? A little girl who was so beautiful, so intelligent, so nice, and who had everything to be happy. She had held on for another two weeks, hovering between life and death, as the girl surely knew; but since, if Gabrielle had lived, she would have remained forever paralyzed, perhaps it had been better this way, perhaps it was better that she had died. To live on in that state, to hope that she would live on in that state "was not fair."

When the girl had finished reading Miss Bell's letter, she tried to revive, inside herself, the days spent in Lisbon. But they seemed to have disappeared forever, along with the colors and fragrances of that swollen and stormy spring. Under her fingers, she seemed to feel Gabrielle's short, soft curls. And before her eyes there arose the image of Ruben, paralyzed. She knew perfectly well that it was not true, and that it was Gabrielle who, had she lived, would have been sitting in a wheel chair. But the girl could not get the image out of her mind, and she continued to see him like that, immobile and alone, a powerful Icarus with broken wings.

ANGELA M. JEANNET

Afterword: Exiles and Returns in Angela Bianchini's Fiction

The traumatic experience of being uprooted because of persecution by a majority group has inspired a significant body of twentieth-century European literature. Works written in Italian have been particularly effective in conveying the experience of anti-Fascists and Jewish people in the face of banishment and extermination. Because circumstances, personal specificities, formal choices, and genres vary, the elaboration of such experiential material has taken different forms, including Ignazio Silone's *Fontamara* (written in 1930), Cesare Pavese's *Il carcere* (written in 1938–39), Carlo Levi's *Cristo si è fermato ad Eboli* (*Christ Stopped at Eboli* [1945]), Natalia Ginzburg's *Tutti i nostri ieri* (*All Our Yesterdays* [1952]) and *Le voci della sera* (*Voices in the Evening* [1961]), and the greater part of Giorgio Bassani's fiction, just to name some of the best known. Prominent among the authors in this vast field is Primo Levi, whose name, unlike most others, has acquired renown in recent years beyond an exclusively Italian readership. The books that established his international reputation are *Se questo è un uomo* (*Survival at Auschwitz* [written in 1945–47]) and *I sommersi e i salvati* (*The Drowned and the Saved* [1986]).

Clearly, the term *exile* and its thematic developments are complex. In Anglo-Saxon literary studies, exile has most often been viewed from the perspective of the host culture. Terry Eagleton's focus on the paradox whereby "the heights of modern English literature have been dominated by foreigners and emigrés" (19) is indicative of that frame of reference. Exile might also be viewed as an "enabling fiction" for writers and critics alike, and can be defined in a supposedly inclusive way: "An exile is someone who inhabits one place and remembers or projects the reality of another" (Seidel ix). However, the emergence of voices from the communities of exiles and marginals has inspired an inversion in point of view. Whether actual or metaphorical, exile is the condition familiar to those who are at odds with their societies, and it can be defined and described from the inside. The variety of the essays contained in Mary Lynn Broe and Angela Ingram's *Women's Writing in Exile* demonstrates the richness of the topic and the interpretive nuances the topic allows, a range that permits the contributors to address geographical and social exile as well as linguistic and literary marginality. One must note, however, a point underlined by the editors of this volume: occasionally, intellectuals may say that they choose estrangement from their own culture, but that does not hold true for the contributors to *Women's Writing in Exile*. Neither is it true – one must assume – for women intellectuals in general, who are "necessarily . . . alien and critical" (3) within a gendered society.

In Angela Bianchini we find yet another variation on the theme of exile and, more importantly, on the theme of return. To begin with, her protagonists are most often women who are both Roman and Jewish – a true nightmare for the Mussolinian mythology of Rome. Their "identities" appear to place them at the center of a culturally well-defined universe: they are Italian and Roman. But Italian culture is far from monolithic. It is not by accident that Jewish Italians who lived outside the far northeastern area of Italy – which was formerly part of a quiltlike conglomerate called the Austro-Hungarian Empire – assumed that their national and cultural integration excluded even the possibility of persecution. To look at one facet of this complex question, it is useful to remember Thomas Harrison's analysis of what he calls "Judaic indeterminacy"(20). The focus of his book is the period preceding a major crisis in southeastern Europe when *identity*, whether political or personal, was a term rife with conflict and uncertainty. Harrison documents how Italian-speaking writers and artists who were subjects of the Austro-Hungarian empire lived that crisis in the most personal and dramatic way. Harrison writes of individuals immersed in a culture of diversity that had steadily been moving toward instability and fragmentation, whereas Bianchini writes of characters faced with a sudden and unexpected loss of a sense of entitlement and innocence.

All exiles are different in spite of their commonalities. Most traumatized perhaps are the exiles who believed they were an integral part of a unitary whole. For Bianchini's characters, one should reverse a phrase from *Women's Writing in Exile*: "Yesterday's place of exile can be tomorrow's center" (2). Their fictional background is the period that extended from the 1930s to the 1950s, as unsettled a time as there ever was. They speak of exile, but their focus is the return to a land they used to call their own, a "center" that remains passionately loved and nostalgically contemplated as if it were forever lost: "Yesterday's center can be tomorrow's place of exile." Exile and return acquire ever wider thematic meaning in Bianchini's later works; Bianchini's characters and narrative style ultimately define an author who looks beyond events, however crucial they may have been in the autobiographical experience, to confirm the complexity of the reciprocal impact between what is lived and what is written. The issue of estrangement, variously defined in each text and accompanied by her characters' efforts to build new connections, and the question of the construction of a female presence, which is seen as a corporeal, emotional, and reflective being-in-history, are revisited in different ways in all of Bianchini's works. Her stories speak of young people's many forms of unawareness, of their being deceived and expropriated, and of their painful but liberating attainment of a level of consciousness that prompts them to reclaim a lost domain.

Departures and exiles in Bianchini's fiction are not explicitly dramatic events; they are periods of suspension between a past state of unawareness and a slowly emerging and unknown future. For her characters the discomfort of dawning awareness lies at first in being suspended in that fluid space between waiting for that future and memory of the past. The Italian word *attesa* reveals the multiple layers in Bianchini's texts. It does not simply indicate *the wait*, or *waiting*, rather flat and uninspiring English words one might have to use in translation, and it is not yet "hope." It is something in between these two conditions of being, something that indicates a suspension in time, in part frightening and in part dimly hopeful. The novella *The Edge of Europe* is the best example of Bianchini's development of the theme of departure: connected closely to the theme of exile as its painful *incipit*, it explores the entering into a new dimension of existence. Written in the third person, *The Edge of Europe* is the story of a young woman whose name is never revealed. She is called *la ragazza*, a name – again – not faithfully translated. Rather than *girl*, the name more closely corresponds to *young woman*, but today this expression in American English has become a bit dated. A distance is thus created between the narrator, who is speaking years after the fact, and the character, who is caught in that traumatic moment of the past. The distance between writer, narrator, and protagonist, on the other hand – a distance that defines what is literary – is effected by the clarity, precision, and directness of the writing: neither shadows nor soft focusing alter the clean lines of the narrative. Emotions are seen in a sharp, immobile light in short episodes that follow one another with a staccato rhythm, and they are conjured up from a past as crystalline as a present.

Seen from the point of view of a later time, the chronology of events stops abruptly when the young woman boards a ship to America; a gaping emptiness takes the place of the years of upcoming exile, years when the pain and fatigue of returning could not even be imagined. The protagonist's keen attention to her environment and her sensitivity to the details of the natural world contrast with her ignorance and slow realization of the complexities of the political and social situation. Each moment the protagonist spends in Lisbon waiting to sail to New York is a step in two directions: one toward recapturing the past that is by now beyond reach and one toward a future that is even more difficult to fathom. In both instances, gaining knowledge is like opening a painful wound. Departure reveals its nature as the beginning of an exile – an exile with ancient roots in human history but with a present face as personal tragedy. For the young woman, the stages of departure are: the journey by air from Rome to Lisbon, away from the false paradise of a country she thought was her own; the loss of her most profoundly possessed and beloved means of communication – the Italian language; her discovery of the social barriers that divide the throngs of refugees; and, most painful of all, her rising sense of guilt when she realizes that because of her ignorance and luck she is perhaps going to be saved, while members of her family and community are left behind. The luxuriant city where the young woman is waiting is "a sort of clinic. A waiting room. After a while, one just can't stand it any more" (*The Edge of Europe* 35; translations are mine). From the beginning of the character's journey, an aspect of the theme of entering into exile is evident – the impossibility of telling other human beings, even the most loved, about one's experience: "for a long time she would not have anyone to whom she could recount the experiences of that day" (11). The reader knows that incommunicability of experience is not a matter of spatial separation. As Primo Levi told us in *Se questo è un uomo* (74–75), *Ad ora incerta* (18), and *I sommersi e i salvati* (4), the recurring nightmare of the persecuted is precisely the impossibility of conveying their experience. The narrator discreetly suggests the compassion she feels for the mixture of truth and naïveté contained in the statement made by her character: the young woman will find it impossible to share more than the events of a few days.

In *Gli oleandri*, which Bianchini wrote in 1962, when the impact of historical events was more recent, the narrator also spoke of exile. But the past evoked in this text is closer than in *The Edge of Europe*, which returns to the beginning of a story of banishment and discovery. Greater space is given in *Gli oleandri* to the protagonist's short-lived attempts to settle in the United States, and then to her return to Rome. The speaker weaves a tale in the first person about the dailiness of living with traumas and the way pain and loss are filtered through memory. The immediacy of the rapport between reader and narrator is built through the technique Bianchini uses to negotiate the conflicting requirements of autobiography, memoir, and fiction. The novella records the burdens the protagonist sustained and the discoveries she made: "leaving, I understood then and never forgot, does not mean going elsewhere, which would be relatively easy; it means not being there, when one knows that things do remain" (*Capo d'Europa* 8). Attempting to erase one's previous life is impossible: "telling oneself that the earlier life had not existed . . .

had been useless . . . however deeply buried, what you were always ends up by resurfacing" (23). What is gone aches in the present, a transitional state exiles try to make livable by filling it with new objects: furniture, people, new habits, and even the attentively observed unfamiliar ceremonies and behaviors of a foreign culture. In-between: that is the place of the exiled, whether or not they make conscious efforts to belong. Even marriage and divorce are evidence of the protagonist's desire to both set roots and to move on again: "suddenly, Charles seemed to have been just a mishap, like the war, like the [racial] laws, like death; it was something that had happened, had hurt, and then was not there any more" (29).

Le nostre distanze, a novel published in 1965, is also set in a world that seems totally divorced from all things past, a world where things past remain alive only in the psyche of the exiled. The alien quality of life on an American university campus isolated like a fortress in the midst of a city that harbors the poor, the dispossessed, and the exiled (who with unintentional irony are called "refugees") makes clear the hopelessness of the character's attempts at finding permanence and a refuge. Scholars may well refuse to give in to the horrors of experience by trusting in lofty commitments, in reason, in loyalty, in literature, in books, but their effort is defeated as failed love stories, nostalgias, existential tragedies, and useless recourses to religions devoid of compassion reveal the precarious situation and solitude of the exiled, even in the campus environment. The arbitrariness of historical events and the unforeseeable direction of their paths, as well as the flaws of the human community, are inimical to the survival of human beings, who are left battered, displaced, and fundamentally alone.

Much written about women's historical narratives increases the complexity of the debates long surrounding the subgenre called historical fiction. No doubt there are multiple reasons why historically grounded fiction consistently fascinates writers and readers alike. The connections with existential concerns, the dramatic quality of the historical events usually selected by the writers, and the intriguing mixture of "true-to-life" and fictional elements usually motivate such predilection. For many women writers, the yearning to evoke the universe of female experience and to place it in the context of human events nourishes an inclination toward history-related narratives. For two comprehensive reviews of this topic as it relates to Italian women writers, it is useful to read Carol Lazzaro-Weis and Graziella Parati. Fiction in which, to borrow Graziella Parati's expression, "public history and private stories" intersect is a favored genre for Italian women writers from the early 1930s on, and this can be tied in many ways to the sociopolitical transformations Italian culture was undergoing at the time. Maria Bellonci, from *Lucrezia Borgia* (*The Life and Times of Lucrezia Borgia* [1939]) to her last work, *Rinascimento privato* (*Private Renaissance* [1985]), favored document-based fiction that rotated around women characters yearning for power and braving danger on the ambiguous border between public scene and private sphere. She appropriated an entire historical era – the Renaissance – and elaborated an original style wherein modernistic emphasis on rhythm, melody, and lexicon was carefully mixed with measured archaic touches. Anna Banti, in novellas and novels such as *Lavinia fuggita* (1951) and *Artemisia* (1947), explored the ways by which her female characters managed to create art while existing on the margins and were able to find a hard-won freedom in that solitude. The formation of these writers was anchored in modernism. For the young Bianchini as well, modernism was the key influence: between 1941 and the 1950s she developed in forced isolation from her cultural, literary, and linguistic milieu.

To understand the work of those who began writing in Italy after 1945, it is useful to remember Italo Calvino's reflections as he looked back at the writing of his own first novel, situated in the Resistance years (*Il sentiero dei nidi di ragno* [*The Path to the Nests of Spiders*]). It was not the so-called neorealism that encouraged the emergence of new writers and of women writers but rather the reverse. The arrival of new voices and the new exploration of the ways in which individuals and communities coped with the turmoil caused by historical events were actually the factors that transformed Italian literary practice. After the long years of silences and the myriad experiences that needed to be shared, everyone who survived the terrible 1940s had a yearning for storytelling, witnessing, and communicating with other people. The only question – said Calvino – seemed to be the choice of modes of narration and styles, since the content appeared to be all there, ready to burst. For some, that meant writing chronicles and autobiographies. For Calvino, the choice was not the confessional, nostalgic mode but a detached posture; for Natalia Ginzburg and Elsa Morante, as different as they are in practice, the focus shifted to the conflict between history, with its cruelty and its aura of self-importance, and the vagaries of individual stories. In the novels by Ginzburg I mentioned earlier and in Morante's *La storia* (*The Story* [1974]) a voice was given to the quiet despair that presided over women's lives. It is significant that in Bianchini's fiction the same conflict becomes a fundamental component of daily existence, even when the war is over and the world seems to harbor no danger or pain. Her thinly veiled autobiographical fiction evolves into an exploration of ways women envision and control their situation in the world. Her voices move from the first person of her early years to the third person of her later work, and autobiography, history, and invention converge, yielding an original text where existential motifs lead toward wider narrative fields.

For Bianchini, women's self-discovery is at the same time an individual acquisition of a new consciousness and a realization of women's own implication in history's events, whose significance and power is revealed to them as they leave childhood. No two experiences of that intersection of the personal and the historical is the same, and Bianchini's fiction subtly exposes the stereotypes and illusions fostered by conventional narratives. For the young woman in *The Edge of Europe*, the diaspora was simply a word as long as she lived in Rome, sheltered by the self-deceptive assumptions made by an entire population (not only Jewish), but during her brief, yet strangely timeless, stopover in Lisbon, the word becomes a reality of frightening magnitude. Connected as the diaspora is to a centuries-old historical dimension and as riddled as it is with existential complexities, it sets apart a group of people and at the same time reproduces in a microcosm the variety of experiences that are part of the world at large. The protagonist comes to realize the contradiction between the utter rigidity and the ephemeral quality of the concept of nationality, a concept that makes possible the enactment of human ferocity. The warmth and security that used to be given her by her sense of belonging to a specific culture are swept away: "the only difference that existed now was between those who were going to leave and those who would stay behind" (*The Edge of Europe* 97). The shock of that realization translates into a sense of loss and disconsolate nostalgia: "This is the Diaspora. . . . This is, for all, the moment of the lights' dimming, the loss of all love and safety. All end in the Diaspora" (82–83).

The concrete image for that sudden discovery of the doom awaiting an entire civilization is the rock that juts into the Atlantic at the extreme southwestern tip of Europe: Cabo da Roca, that "strip of land hemmed in between a Europe abandoned to persecutors and victims, and the ocean that hid submarines under its waves" (59). The protagonist goes to visit the cape on a stormy day. Beyond Lisbon, a noble and elegant city recovering from the violence of a wind that left "a sort of time vacuum that only the storm could now fill," (57) lies the dark promontory, forbidding and tormented by the battering of the waves: "These rocks were black – eaten by the waves that penetrated deep inside them with foam, reflected light, and high sprays. And they were corroded by the ocean, even though they rose up like a bastion, as in obstinate resistance . . . sunken, invisible, gone – only to resurface again, no longer sea water, but earth and rock" (60). Other writers, from Matthew Arnold to Eugenio Montale, had seen in the ocean's assaults on the land the image of an immense tragedy, and they turned the desolate and stormy landscape into a metaphor for the demise of an entire culture. But in Bianchini it is a young girl, one among the innocent and excluded, who gives new vividness to this trope as she becomes aware at the same time of that tragedy – her exclusion – and of a sense of cruel and incomprehensible betrayal. As soon as she boards the ship sailing toward safety, her resolution is to not look upon Europe anymore.

And yet, beyond the sorrowful perspective forced on her by events, the protagonist of *The Edge of Europe* discovers the resourcefulness of human beings and comes to admire the cosmopolitan quality of a group of Jewish people who lack permanent roots, who are aware, who fight against political foes and fate, and who are constantly on the move – those who come from all over Europe and whom the narrator felicitously defines as "aristocrats of departures and nostalgias" (49). The most vivid character in *The Edge of Europe* is Juan Ruben, a middle-aged man of many names and faces who works feverishly at providing safe passage to as many of his people as possible. He is surrounded by an unconventional set of family members, and at first he reminds the protagonist of a romantic film hero, a young Jean Gabin. It is only toward the end of her brief sojourn in Lisbon, among the commotion of masses of refugees attempting to flee, that Ruben loses his romantic halo and becomes "real" for the young woman as a very contradictory man: crafty and tender, pragmatic and humorous, pursued by the specter of untold tragedies, and yet able to indulge in the pleasures of life. In contact with him and his family, the young woman begins to see how the privileges of a conventional bourgeois existence had distanced her from the plight of earlier refugees who had fled Germany and Eastern Europe and had begged well-to-do Roman Jews for help in their flight (89–90). She also realizes that the limited scope of her vision had prevented her from understanding the dangers of Fascism and the hollow quality of nationalistic pieties. She discovered a human connection with those she had once ignored, and she was intrigued by the man with "his thickset frame and his olive complexion, . . . Middle-Eastern rather than French" (33).

Even though the young woman's passage through Lisbon takes place in a dreamlike atmosphere – a mysterious limbo with sharply detailed scenes – the characters are entirely credible and realistic. All the characters in this novella, as well as in the rest of Bianchini's work, are drawn with precision of touch, and, even though they are filtered through another character's memory, they are never transformed into mythical figures; they are complex and filled with contradictions.

This was already true in earlier texts. For instance, in *Le nostre distanze*, the fictional image of Ted Baldwin, a handsome graduate student on the barely disguised Johns Hopkins campus, stands out as an outcast among a rather large set of characters obviously drawn from life. Baldwin is tormented by his inability to cope with his homosexuality and the cruelty of a rejecting society. His controlled gestures and obsessive speech patterns, his need for human contact at the same time sought and refused, and his ultimate defeat as he retreats into the rigid and compassionless world of conventions make him an unforgettable character.

In *Gli oleandri*, the story of the protagonist is paralleled by the story of Orietta, the protagonist's childhood friend and in many ways her mirror image. The protagonist left Rome, but her friend remained; one was Jewish and persecuted, while the other was involved, however unwittingly, with Fascists; one survives and returns, the other dies and disappears. The bond between the two endures through the years, and when the unnamed protagonist learns of her friend's tragic end, the reader is inevitably reminded of a Pavesian character with a similar fate. In *La luna e i falò*, Cesare Pavese gives to a capricious young girl involved in dangerous games between Fascists and Resistance fighters the function of a mythical figure, whose very name – Santa – denotes her "sacred" quality. In the Pavesian universe all the female characters are members of an alien race, the "razza puttana delle donne" ("the whorish race of women") always too eager for sex (*Opere* 491, 503, and passim), and men would rather stay away from them (392 and passim). Santa's killing and subsequent burning are a consequence not only of her being the symbol of a time and place crazed by political hate but also a rite of purification and an exorcism, because she embodies all the seductive, dangerous, and repellent qualities of her gender, as the witches of old did. The bonfire that used to be lit in ancient times, not on fields but on uncultivated land, in a ritual meant to rid the countryside of malignant presences destroys even the last remnant of Santa's body.

Nothing of the sort is in Bianchini's text. The whimsical, beautiful girl who shared the protagonist's childhood games of make-believe relives in the memory and compassion of her friend as a woman with qualities, flaws, and family secrets, a young woman who made her own choices. The survivor's pain of losing her is assuaged by the voice of the man who is the narrator's new love: "living . . . is always a bit like those dresses of your childhood. You cut them, you sew them, you try them on, you adorn them, you work on them until they fit you beautifully, until you believe they fit you beautifully, until they are completely ours. That dress, her life . . . Orietta had it, and it fit her, it was hers" (*Capo d'Europa* 90). Orietta is redeemed not by a quasi-pagan sacrifice, like Pavese's Santa, but by her friend's acknowledgment of her desire to find her dream and define her own life. The imperceptible transition from *vostri* (yours) to *nostro* (ours), from a second- to a first-person plural, makes the speaker's reflection inclusive, and by so doing reinserts Orietta's tormented life into a context that one refuses to judge.

Return in Italian literature is often return to a city. Large or small, it is a place with deeply rooted and instantly recognizable characteristics. In Bianchini's fiction, that city is Rome. The mythological image of Rome as the nurturing city is many centuries old. What initially sets apart this author's treatment of the image is that the voices speaking in her fiction are those of young women – a choice that allows the maternal icon to be reclaimed from the sons' realm of political ideologies, whether of ancient Rome, the Risorgimento, or Fascism. In addition, the characters share an intense, sensuous intimacy with the city in spite of their long absences due to what can only be construed as rejection by that same city. Rome represents all that was believed eternal, all that was lost, and all that remains as unquenched nostalgia. Roman life is the "center" forever threatened and, paradoxically, the most poignant reminder of exile. Innumerable glimpses of a beloved urban environment mark Bianchini's pages: a street full of shops, with an ancient church at its end, and a luminosity reflected from the church's stained-glass windows; the humid earth of the parks surrounding Roman villas, fragrant and covered with flowers and wild grasses among the marble statues and ruins; a suspension in the air; a sky filled with blue, and immensely deep; and the various seasons, caught in their specific charm, whether the time is spring, December, or summer.

The prodigy of the city's presence has to do as much with its air as with the signs of a bygone grandeur: "It was a warm and empty Sunday afternoon, and the city seemed to be combed by sirocco breezes that rustled in the treetops along the silent avenues" (36). Above all, Bianchini makes visible and audible the presence of people in the streets, squares, and parks of Rome. But even in the evocation of love lived in the urban summer nights, the city appears familiar in its vastness and emptiness, with avenues like rivers, park benches like jetties, and streetcars like mysterious ships touching the shores of a small island. In her novel titled *Le labbra tue sincere*, set in 1910, Rome is the true protagonist. It is the Rome that in 1870 had become the capital of a new political entity, for better and for worse, but it is also the Rome that was a metaphor for an entire culture's inchoate desire, a desire that would later be so cleverly exploited by Mussolini. It is the ambivalent quality of this city, at the same time irretrievably lost and eternal in its sensuous magnificence, that lends intensity to the secret passion shared by the man and the woman who are at the center of the novel.

Bianchini's *ragazze* invariably return to Rome, but theirs are strange returns. The protagonist of *Gli oleandri* even says that "she felt that she had returned to Italy an infinite number of times" (*Capo d'Europa* 30). However, within that recapturing of a city's charm and of the memories stored in it, another presence would always transpire in sudden and almost imperceptible ways – the loneliness of the great cities of the eastern United States and the colors and smells and sounds of America: "the breeze carried the powerful scents of honeysuckle and laurel, of linden blossoms and broom, but mixed with them was . . . the burning, humid breath of an early

American summer in the faraway Continent" (204). The dimension of "other" cannot be erased, and each protagonist lives in a sort of suspended time/space, aware of her situation as a "mixed blood." The "racially" motivated persecution that caused the banishment and exclusion of Bianchini's characters has brought to light a deeper estrangement. That sense of precariousness rooted in having a double or multiple cultural identity becomes part of her characters' consciousness. Permanence is illusory, the fallacy of wholeness is due to self-delusion or ignorance, and love for a place is always and inevitably accompanied by nostalgia for a sense of certainty and safety that cannot be retrieved. Connections must be built with the certainty that they will be life-giving, intense, but temporary – destined to dissolve in time: "she had to face the impossibility of possessing the firm support she had been taught to believe in" (330). This is why Bianchini's protagonists are wrapped in their peculiar solitude. As she contemplates the melancholy beauty of Villa Borghese and the ancient meadows dotted with trees and ruins, a young woman reflects: "There are moments one feels like that. Life seems to have ended a long time ago, and death seems not to have yet decided to come . . . a breeze had begun to blow, almost cold, among the oaks and the pines, over the fountains and the meadows" (63). Estrangement and irreducible exile become fundamental elements of the protagonist's life in *La ragazza in nero*. No matter what the circumstances of her past may have been, "she did not find, she would not be able to find anyone she knew, even though she had spent her entire life in that city" (198). At the same time, especially in her later writings, Bianchini develops a metonymic relationship between her characters and their city. The novella titled *La ragazza in nero* includes four generations of women. The central character is again called *la ragazza*, but her baby daughter has a name, and a very Roman one at that: Prisca. Its reference to archaic Latinity – its deep roots in an ancient civilization – makes it clear that the young mother has relinquished her tenuous hold on her own name while she simultaneously attempts to create connections. The young woman's mother, *la Mamma*, is extremely tormented, and, in her relationship with her daughter, she went through the stages familiar to many mothers: after being the object of her little girl's adoration, she became the target of adolescent hostility and incomprehension. It is the complex image of a youthful and elegant grandmother, *la Nonna*, that sums up all the beauty and humanness of the city: she is mature, sensual, and sophisticated, yet maternal and tender. Her presence, filtered through the memory of her admiring granddaughter and glimpsed or evoked in sudden apparitions that recur in the nonlinear pattern of the narration, brings a sense of serenity and longing to the story. Her passionate but discreet relationship with a younger man informs the young girl's *éducation sentimentale* and also her discovery of sensuality. The joy of physical and emotional well-being shines through the grandmother's features: "Her happiness was reflected in her luminous eyes, her radiant face, and her softly harmonious voice" (131). The backdrop to the bond between *la Nonna* and *la ragazza* is the city in its daily and seasonal transformations: "[She] would disappear with her quick step, her slender, ageless silhouette, along the darkening paths now shot through by the slanted rays of the setting sun. She was going toward the sunset, with its glorious reds and violets; she was going toward the vast city that was lying just on the other side, beyond the park gates; she was going toward an elsewhere that for her, who was a child, was named just Enzo. The little girl felt a tormenting and ferocious yearning, as for a paradise that one day would be hers by rights" (124). When the moment for loneliness comes, *la Nonna* accepts the inevitable with stoic dignity: "she bore the signs of devastation, but also of love enjoyed. Although aching and wounded, she still had her impetus, her fury" (136). As she soberly enters a new phase in her life, she teaches her granddaughter the inescapable truth: "It was all about growing old well. No one is eternal. Love least of all." (138). Love for a city filtered through the portrayal of a mature woman who is desirable and desiring, and who confronts the arrival of old age with sadness but also dignity and courage, is seldom found in fiction.

Bianchini's originality lies also in the affinity between women and Rome. In order to find a vision comparable to hers, the reader must look to the turn of the century and to the work of a writer we feel is congenial with Bianchini: Colette. For Colette it was Paris that embodied all the seductions of a female and mature being. Paris lives in total symbiosis with the characters of her fiction, beautiful and ripe, elegant and worldly. The maternal, redefined by Colette outside the conventional domestic "scene," truly a constructed stage, is the manifestation of the twin power of sensuality and nurturing. The reflective sensuality of Colette's characters envelops equally children and lovers and male and female friends exactly like the atmosphere of a beloved city (see in particular *Mitsou* [1919], *Chéri* [1920], and *La fin de Chéri* [1926], as well as many of her short stories).

Even beyond Colette's antecedent, Bianchini's fictional universe and writing are profoundly influenced by late-nineteenth- and early-twentieth-century literature. The most obvious point of contact is Bianchini's distinguishing characteristic: her definition of memory and selection of the means by which human beings counteract the action of passing time and forgetfulness. Memory, for her, is an imprint left on the senses; remembering is entrusted to the wisdom of the body. In turn, in the tradition of turn-of-the-century European literature, the function and goal of the conscious effort that produces narration and writing is to bring back to life the memories preserved by the senses: "And then there were other sunsets from the earlier past. She is a little girl at the café with Nonna, or with Nonna and Mamma, or even with Enzo and Nonna, and there is always an ice cream, and a glass of water, and a spoon immersed in the glass; and the Western breeze that would rise and rustle in the leaves, like a sudden warning about passing time" (169). One may naturally think of Proust but also of the Symbolists, and one can even detect in these lines a Keatsean suggestion. The past and its apparent loss are represented through the evocation of never fully erased sensations: the fragrance of oleander blossoms in the story by that title, the sight of the trees along Rome's avenues, "a bit dusty and shaken by the summer wind" (32), the colors of American sunsets, and the sounds around New York's Penn Station. Bianchini's protagonists are storehouses of sensations. Even the betrayals of memory are experienced as physical phenomena: "For too long a time I had breathed the fragrance of oleanders, or believed that I had; now, no fragrance could be detected any more" (11).

The evocation of human beings is also entrusted to the memory of the senses, and here again we find in Bianchini the echoes of a sensibility nourished by a turn-of-the-century literature that understood clothing as more than covering for the body, and elegance as more than superficial obedience to fashion. The pastel colors the grandmother wore, her suede shoes, the "white felt hats with the brim slightly raised on one side" (104), the silk dress "stupendous, all lilac and pink nuances" (136), and her fragrance, tender and discreet, define the woman who lives on at the core of a young woman's universe. Clothing is not simply a display for the male gaze either; it is a system of signs that establishes a connection between women and marks significant moments in the life of the protagonist. When *la ragazza* faces a fundamental transformation in her life, its harbinger is a young woman dressed in black, who, wearing a wide-brimmed black hat and a black velvet jacket, first seems to be a specter emerging from the fog shrouding a city park. Later, after her pregnancy and delivery, when *la ragazza* again becomes sensitive to the seductions of life, the attainment of her new status is revealed by her delight in the beauty and softness of young girls' fashions: "tender colors never seen before, the softest grey, a camel with noisette and sand nuances, dazzling black, a red all fantasy and flame, a special pink . . . colors, nuances to be tasted sensuously, like ice cream cones, with eager tongue, to evoke unexpected sensations that still had a flavor of nostalgia and memory" (211–12).

Exile, estrangement, and the powerful yet precarious reality of connections and returns emerge in *La ragazza in nero* as part of a more specifically female experience. *La ragazza's* story, while having in the background the memory of an American period and therefore an objective distance and a physical return to a place once lost, has to do with another sort of transition into adulthood: the choice she makes to enter alone the realm of maternity. The novella includes the dreams of the young woman and her relationship, as desired as it is temporary, with a young man. Every episode of her life leads toward a new definition of her own existence and toward the enactment of a project – to have her own child – that will take her out of her limbolike adolescence. In order to reach the other shore after her existential "passage," however, she must first experience separation from the other *ragazze*. As she becomes totally absorbed in the baby she has borne, she lives "in a sort of apartheid that reminded her of her years in the American school, when she acted as if she were exactly like all the other little girls" (100). Even vis-à-vis her family, her becoming "different" – a single mother – means estrangement: "When she was with the three of them, who were unchanged and unaware . . . she felt truly anguish at her future condition of exile and marginalization " (160). She sees the old ties and cohesion dissolve in spite of her family's lack of criticism of her life choice. When she and her baby move to a small but comfortable apartment, her sense of setting off adrift toward the unknown is expressed, significantly, by metaphors taken from sea journeys: "At times, she had the sensation that the building creaked in the midst of a gale . . . on that stormy ocean, she and Prisca were almost shipwrecked, at the mercy of a small raft that offered little protection" (192). Yet the energy-laden joy of return beckons. As she looks at herself in a mirror, *la ragazza* sees the past disappear in a violent burst: "A sweeping wind was blowing over ruins and regrets. She heard a voice, a call to live" (193). With the term *giustiziere* that speaks of a judgment, redress, and total erasure, the young woman looks upon her past as an obscure trial, due not to events willed by human beings but to life itself. Only an overpowering life urge can defeat existential cruelty and sweep it away, at least temporarily. Certainly, there is something romantic and modernistic in this impulse and in the character's reassertion of a will to live. The bonds between successive generations of women – grandmother, mother, daughter, *ragazza in nero*, and then baby daughter – however problematic, indicate the possibility of connections and enduring, which find their expression in the young woman's voluptuous listening to the transformations her body undergoes.

A woman's body "so rich in signs" (Magli 6) is at the center of *La ragazza in nero*, and this attention gives the novella its specificity as well as its relevance in the context of today's debates about women's writing wherein Bianchini would occupy a singular place. Her text never explicitly challenges a gendered universe of experience and writing. Yet, it consistently explores the corporeal presence of women in the world, and "the place we accord it" (Suleiman 1). Bianchini's writing simultaneously pursues distance and participation, bending with ease the tools made available by the Italian written tradition so that they serve her own vision. Women, for Bianchini, are both the surveyors of the domain of the body and the domain surveyed, as they reclaim a variety of female experiences, and reappropriate their physical selves. In chapter 3, which is pivotal in the novella, the appearance of the "girl in black," accompanied by a cherublike little son, in the midst of a lovingly described park of the Roman Villa Borghese is a puzzling apparition even for the protagonist. She is drawn with precise, realistic touches, yet remains mysterious and spectral – "a bit Medusa and a bit sybilla" (*Capo d'Europa* 124). The passing reference to mythical female figures associated with magic and the prophetic spirit heightens the suspense and dreamlike quality of the episode. The *ragazza in nero* is a sign foreboding a life passage; she seems to fathom, in her uncanny, direct way, the physical and emotional situation of the protagonist. A commonplace encounter with a mother and her child in a city park becomes a contact with mystery. Around the visitor, the shadows of a miragelike past appear and disappear softly: the grounds once rich in pristine beauty, the children who once set small boats adrift in the clear ponds, and the grandmother, now gone, in the years of her happiness. The entire episode, with its quiet intensity, fog-shrouded landscape, and suspense, is the metaphor for a ritual immersion in another world, which the body tells in its own language: "a mild languor . . . was flowing under her skin, at times stronger, almost painful, and at times barely perceptible; it ran along her legs, down her calves and to her ankles, like a river that brought fertility inside her, making her a bit sick and listless, yet somehow more alive" (114). The desire to have a child is marked by the protagonist's attention to that language. She enjoys her (perhaps) last menstruation as "a shore she was about to abandon" (145), and starts making careful calculations about what is happening in the darkness inside her. "[I]n that humble female arithmetic" is something poised ambiguously between planning and adventure, "something heartbreaking and voluptuous." (158).

Prisca is born, and a new life begins with that "gift . . . the only one that she had given herself in all her life . . . it had the perfection of an exam successfully taken and of love enjoyed" (175). The baby's presence does bring together the three women – mother, grandmother, and *ragazza* – but this "return" is neither the happy closure of traditional narratives nor the secure establishment of a female genealogy (for the development of the concept of female genealogies by one of its major proponents, Luce Irigaray, see *Engaging with Irigaray*, edited by Carolyn Burke, Naomi Schor, and Margaret

Whitford). The novella ends not with the promise of enduring women's domains even in the acknowledgment of powerful bonds but rather in the evidence of the protagonist's readiness to mature and to face solitude, a serene revisitation of the past and a leave-taking from what cannot be retrieved: "Prisca . . . had all of a sudden become herself as a child; that childhood had already been lived and known, they were beginning to go through it again, together, along a familiar path. . . . Prisca was herself with her mother, in an undefined moment of time, a sort of free zone . . . a combination of solitude and mutual solidarity" (202). The conclusion brings together the various strands of the sinuous narration. A glimpse of the *ragazza in nero* waiting at a bus stop, caught by the protagonist as she drives by, awakens desire – "that ancient and hard companion of a lifetime" (197). *La ragazza* greets with hesitancy and surprise her renewed attention to the sensuality of clothing (211), a feeling that accompanies another feeling that anything can happen, after her mourning for what is not anymore. The story closes on the innocent seductiveness of a teenaged clothing-store clerk extolling the new spring fashions, and a thought of Prisca: "Prisca . . . had to have a dress. She was a big girl, now, and [her mother] could already picture her round knees peeking from under the hem" (219).

To draw the world of her imagination, Bianchini relies on a stylistic model that privileges concision and understatement. She is well aware of one's "duty to form" (Corona 191) in the creation of a tradition of women's writing, and her work is a further demonstration of how different the voices of women writers are (Lazzaro-Weis xi) and how complex the paths toward fashioning them. Bianchini's texts are enriched by the tension of things left unsaid, and the short episodes she favors are like snapshots, intense and vivid, with a margin of mystery. In *Gli oleandri*, the episodes are mingled in a forward and back pattern, as the protagonist works at recapturing confused and dispersed fragments of lives. In *The Edge of Europe* the chapters, at times just two pages long, are placed in exact chronological order, as images in a photo album. This choice aptly induces the desired distancing effect and at the same time accentuates, by hiding them behind the orderly pattern of narration, the terror and pain of the protagonist's situation. *The Edge of Europe*, told in the third person, constructs a character who remains unnamed, but whose every instant is known to the unidentified narrator. In *La ragazza in nero*, the narration moves in waves, imitating the water's back-and-forth flow.

Because of Bianchini's power of observation but also because she selects qualifiers that surprise the reader, sceneries and psychologies emerge vividly in each of her works. The adjectives she chooses rely on swift and sensuous metonymies and are often audaciously paired. For instance, the personality of a beloved friend shines through her handwriting: "that handwriting of hers, rounded but daring and clear" (*Capo d'Europa* 22); the feeling elicited by a welcome season is caught in a way that is rich and exact: "that tender and ripe season" (303); and a flower just blossoming is "ripe with beauty" (133).

Although her prose is informed by women's experiences, Bianchini uses with skill and nonchalance the tools of the "fathers" for her purposes. Her writing is controlled yet not self-reflexive. It is quintessentially classic yet conveys a sense of immediacy, thanks to the author's ability to interpret the life of the senses, a life that is powerful, rich in wisdom, and impossible to repress. To borrow Maria Rosa Cutrufelli's words, we find a perspective that is "a message that . . . suggests the long research women have embarked upon, the sense of their handing down a wealth of experiences, and their complex, often painful, elaboration of reality" (in Corona 255). Bianchini's characters, between exile and return, between estrangement and awareness, address and exorcise "the issue of solitude" (*Voce donna* x) and look upon life as a construction of their own selves. Like dresses – those objects as intimate as a skin and so lovingly made – that are designed to fit women's bodies with meditated precision, creation of personal identities is not fixed or predetermined but is patterned with and against the events.

WORKS CITED

Bianchini, Angela. *Capo d'Europa*. Milan: Bompiani, 1992. Includes a revised version of *Gli oleandri*, *La ragazza in nero*, and *Capo d'Europa*, all of which were first published separately by Camunia editrice (Milan: 1962, 1990, 1991).

———. *Le labbra tue sincere*. Milan: Frassinelli, 1995.

———. *Lungo equinozio*. Milan: Lerici, 1962. Includes *Gli oleandri*, *Festa dell'indipendenza*, and *Lungo equinozio*.

———. *Le nostre distanze*. Milan: Mondadori, 1965.

———. *Voce donna*. 1979. Milan: Frassinelli, 1996.
Broe, Mary Lynn, and Angela Ingram, eds. *Women's Writing in Exile*. Chapel Hill: U North Carolina P, 1989.
Burke, Carolyn, Naomi Schor, and Margaret Whitford, eds. *Engaging with Irigaray*. New York: Columbia UP, 1994
Calvino, Italo. *Il sentiero dei nidi di ragno*. Turin: Einaudi, 1964.
Corona, Daniela, ed. *Donne e scrittura*. Palermo: La Luna, 1990.
Eagleton, Terry. *Exiles and Emigrés*. New York: Schocken, 1970.
Harrison, Thomas. 1910. *The Emancipation of Dissonance*. Berkeley: U California P, 1996.
Lazzaro-Weis, Carol. *From Margins to Mainstream: Feminism and Fictional Modes in Italian Women's Writing, 1968–1990*. Philadelphia: U Pennsylvania P, 1993.
Levi, Primo. *Ad ora incerta*. Milan: Garzanti, 1990.
———. *Se questo è un uomo*. "Nuovi Coralli." Turin: Einaudi, 1971.
———. *I sommersi e i salvati*. Turin: Einaudi, 1986.
Magli, Patrizia, ed. *Le donne e i segni: Scrittura, linguaggio, identità nel segno della differenza femminile*. Luoghi Comuni 1. Ancona: Lavoro Editoriale, 1985.
Parati, Graziella. *Public Histories, Private Stories*. Minneapolis: U Minnesota P, 1996.
Pavese, Cesare. *Opere*. Turin: Einaudi, 1961.
Seidel, Michael. *Exile and the Narrative Imagination*. New Haven: Yale UP 1986.
Suleiman, Susan, ed. *The Female Body in Western Culture*. Cambridge: Harvard UP, 1985.

GLOSSARY

Ala Littoria Name of the Italian national airline during the Fascist regime.

Alpine Corps In Italian the word *alpini* refers to those army troops who specialize in mountain battles.

American First A political group in the United States that opposed intervention on the side of the Allies.

Ara Pacis Literally, the "altar of peace." A monument in Rome erected in 13 BC to celebrate the victories of Augustus in Spain and Gaul as well as the arrival of peace in all the Roman dominions.

Azaña y Díaz, Manuel A Spanish politician and supporter of the unified Leftist parties who was elected president (1936) of the Republic of Spain, an office he held until the Fascist forces of Francisco Franco defeated him.

Balalaika A film that played in Lisbon in 1941 whose name is derived from the name of a stringed musical instrument traditionally associated with the culture of Ukraine.

Bund A short term for the German-American Volksbund, an American group that supported the German Nazis.

Cabo da Roca Near Lisbon, this cape of land marks the western-most portion of the European land mass; understood since antiquity as one end of the known world.

C'est ici que je suis A French expression that translates literally as "It is here that I am."

Churchill, Winston (1874–1965). British politician initially sympathetic to Italian Fascism but who changed his mind and went so far as to predict the possibility of world conflict due to Germany's rearmament.

De Gaulle, Charles (1890–1970). French politician who opposed the armistice with the invading German armies signed by Philippe Pétain and sought refuge in Great Britain, where he launched a massive appeal to the French people asking them to resist the occupying Nazi forces.

diaspora A term derived from the Greek words meaning the "scattering of seed." In general, it refers to the dispersion of any people forced to leave their homeland. In Jewish history, *diaspora* refers to the loss, in antiquity, of a Jewish homeland in the Middle East.

Eden, (Robert) Anthony (1897–1977). British politician who became Britain's foreign minister in 1935 and resigned this post in 1938 in response to Neville Chamberlain's policy of appeasement toward Hitler. Prime Minister, 1955–1957.

Jewish Community Referred to in the original Italian as *la comunità israelitica*, the adjective *israelitico* carries neither the disparaging connotations of the Italian *ebreo* nor the political implications of *israeliano*, a term that refers to the modern state of Israel (not founded until 1948).

mistral The French name given to a wind that also blows in Italy, from the north-northeast, and that is associated with the passing of cold fronts and storms.

navicert The most important document required for safe emigration from Europe to the United States.

Philosopher's Way A pathway that overlooks the city of Heidelberg, Germany, and the Neckar River.

Snow White and the Seven Dwarfs American filmmaker Walt Disney's animated masterpiece released in the United States in 1937 and subsequently released throughout Europe.

Zangwill, Israel (1864–1926). A British author active in the Zionist movement and one of the principal authors of Jewish literature in English. His works include "Children of the Ghetto" (1892), *King of the Schnorrers* (1894), and "Dreamers of the Ghetto" (1898).

Principal source: *Enciclopedia Zanichelli* (Bologna: Zanichelli, 1996)

In the European Women Writers series

Artemisia
By Anna Banti
Translated by Shirley D'Ardia Caracciolo

Bitter Healing: German Women Writers, 1700–1830
An Anthology
Edited by Jeannine Blackwell and Susanne Zantop

The Edge of Europe
By Angela Bianchini
Translated by Angela M. Jeannet and David Castronuovo

The Maravillas District
By Rosa Chacel
Translated by d. a. démers

Memoirs of Leticia Valle
By Rosa Chacel
Translated by Carol Maier

There Are No Letters Like Yours: The Correspondence of Isabelle de Charrière and Constant d'Hermenches
By Isabelle de Charrière
Translated and with an introduction and annotations by Janet Whatley and Malcolm Whatley

The Book of Promethea
By Hélène Cixous
Translated by Betsy Wing

The Terrible but Unfinished Story of Norodom Sihanouk, King of Cambodia
By Hélène Cixous
Translated by Juliet Flower MacCannell, Judith Pike, and Lollie Groth

The Governor's Daughter
By Paule Constant
Translated by Betsy Wing

Maria Zef
By Paola Drigo
Translated by Blossom Steinberg Kirschenbaum

Woman to Woman
By Marguerite Duras and Xavière Gauthier
Translated by Katharine A. Jensen

Hitchhiking: Twelve German Tales
By Gabriele Eckart
Translated by Wayne Kvam

The South and Bene
By Adelaida García Morales
Translated and with a preface by Thomas G. Deveny

The Tongue Snatchers
By Claudine Herrmann
Translated by Nancy Kline

The Panther Woman: Five Tales from the Cassette Recorder
By Sarah Kirsch
Translated by Marion Faber

Concert
By Else Lasker-Schüler
Translated by Jean M. Snook

Slander
By Linda Lê
Translated by Esther Allen

Daughters of Eve: Women's Writing from the German Democratic Republic
Translated and edited by Nancy Lukens and Dorothy Rosenberg

Animal Triste
By Monika Maron
Translated by Brigitte Goldstein

Celebration in the Northwest
By Ana María Matute
Translated by Phoebe Ann Porter

On Our Own Behalf: Women's Tales from Catalonia
Edited by Kathleen McNerney

Dangerous Virtues
By Ana María Moix
Translated and with an afterword by Margaret E. W. Jones

The Forbidden Woman
By Malika Mokeddem
Translated by K. Melissa Marcus

Absent Love: A Chronicle
By Rosa Montero
Translated by Cristina de la Torre and Diana Glad

The Delta Function
By Rosa Montero
Translated and with an afterword by Kari Easton and Yolanda Molina Gavilán

The Life and Adventures of Trobadora Beatrice as Chronicled by Her Minstrel Laura: A Novel in Thirteen Books and Seven Intermezzos
By Irmtraud Morgner
Translated by Jeanette Clausen
With an introduction by Jeanette Clausen and Silke von der Emde

Nadirs
By Herta Müller
Translated and with an introduction by Sieglinde Lug

Music from a Blue Well
By Torborg Nedreaas
Translated by Bibbi Lee

Nothing Grows by Moonlight
By Torborg Nedreaas
Translated by Bibbi Lee

Bordeaux
By Soledad Puértolas
Translated by Francisca González-Arias

Candy Story
By Marie Redonnet
Translated by Alexandra Quinn

Forever Valley
By Marie Redonnet
Translated by Jordan Stump

Hôtel Splendid
By Marie Redonnet
Translated by Jordan Stump

Nevermore
By Marie Redonnet
Translated by Jordan Stump

Rose Mellie Rose
By Marie Redonnet
Translated by Jordan Stump

The Man in the Pulpit: Questions for a Father
By Ruth Rehmann
Translated by Christoph Lohmann and Pamela Lohmann

Abelard's Love
By Luise Rinser
Translated by Jean M. Snook

Why Is There Salt in the Sea?
By Brigitte Schwaiger
Translated by Sieglinde Lug

The Same Sea As Every Summer
By Esther Tusquets
Translated and with an afterword by Margaret E. W. Jones

Never to Return
By Esther Tusquets
Translated and with an afterword by Barbara F. Ichiishi

The Life of High Countess Gritta von Ratsinourhouse
By Bettine von Arnim and Gisela
von Arnim Grimm
Translated and with an introduction by Lisa Ohm

The Edge of Europe